THE SECRETS WE KEEP

M. I. HATTERSLEY

INKUBATOR
BOOKS

Published by Inkubator Books
www.inkubatorbooks.com

ISBN (eBook): 978-1-83756-155-1
ISBN (Paperback): 978-1-83756-156-8
ISBN (Hardback): 978-1-83756-157-5

1

Even with four cups of strong coffee inside me, I'm struggling to focus. My skin is like paper and my teeth feel brittle and unclean. This, despite the fact I've flossed and liberally brushed them before tonight's service. Missing sleep always hit me hard, even when I was a younger man, but add to that the bad dreams and all the other shit going on right now, and it's left my mind swirling in a frenzy of confusion and unhelpful ideas.

Unhelpful?

Try dangerous. Try terrifying.

I lean over the dish and complete the final touches – a selection of sea herbs that are applied around the side of the generous piece of wild turbot with a pair of medical tweezers. Stepping back, I force a smile for Pearl, my sous chef, who has been trying her best to follow the process. She smiles back, but the creased brows tell me she's going to need both practice and guidance if she's to master my signature dish. But it's not her fault. Tonight I'm rushing and being sloppy, going against all my principles on how one should run a high-end kitchen.

How we do anything is how we do everything.

It's a good rule for business. It's a better rule for how to live life.

If only I'd known that twenty years ago.

"It looks beautiful, Chef," Pearl says. "You've smashed it again."

"Do you trust you can handle this tonight?" I ask, ramping up the hopefulness in my voice.

"Erm. Yeah. I might need some help with the champagne foam."

I nod. "Okay."

She's not there yet. But that's fine. She will be. It was never the plan for me to hand over the reins to her so soon, anyway. Mine and Jessie's plan was we'd open the restaurant – me as head chef and her running front-of-house – elevate it up to the best standards possible, maybe get a Michelin star, get a rosette at least, then we'd get the right people in the top roles and take a step back. Enjoy the fruits of our labour. But that was ten years down the line in our original plan. Not three.

There's nothing like an unexpected pregnancy to ruin every single one of your plans.

"Do your best," I tell Pearl, stifling a yawn. "You need to trust yourself. You're an excellent chef."

"Thank you, Rob – Chef!" she says. "I'll do my best."

"I know you will. That's all I can ask of you." I pat her on the shoulder. She'll need a few months of mentoring before the time is right for her. But a few months might be all we've got left here. And it's not like I can afford to take a step back now, anyway. Baby Noah's arrival three weeks ago might have thrown mine and Jessie's lives into a tailspin, but the financial crisis, coming so soon after the pandemic, means the restaurant's finances are teetering on a knife edge. There's no way I can pay a head chef's salary for Pearl and hire another sous chef for the foreseeable future. No matter how hard Jessie is finding it at home on her own looking after a three-week-old baby and our four-year-old, Fern – no matter how much she begs me to slow down and be at home more – I can't do it. Not yet. I'm needed here. If I don't make Fire and Ice work, we'll lose everything. The restaurant, the house, our livelihoods. I can't tell Jessie any of this, of course. I don't want to worry her. She has enough to deal with. But don't we all?

I leave my station and walk down the short passageway that leads out into the dining room. I've always felt restaurants have a strange atmosphere at this time of night. We open in forty-five minutes and an expectant air hangs over the finely laid out tables and chairs. It also feels slightly sinister tonight. Like a tableau from an old film. That bit in the Shining when Jack meets the phantom barman. Or as if it's the dining room on the Titanic, laid out for a dinner service that will never take place.

But perhaps this is just how it looks when filtered through my current frame of mind. I walk over to the bar area and grab a coffee cup from under the counter. It's a little dusty, but clean enough. I walk it over to the new industrial-sized coffee machine in black and chrome that stands proudly in the corner against the back wall. Proudly, but arrogantly. Mocking in its extravagance. We had it imported all the way from Italy and it cost more than my first car. I'm already regretting buying it. I made the final payment just before the first lockdown, and it lay dormant and unused for six months. All the while, everyone in the industry ran around like crazy people, trying to work out how to stay afloat and relevant whilst surviving on the government handouts that barely covered rent and wages.

I switch on the machine and catch sight of myself, reflected in the shiny chrome facade. I look tired and ugly. But that's no surprise. That's how I feel inside.

It's the dreams that do it. I thought they'd stopped, but for whatever reason last night and the night before, I had the same dream.

It's always the same dream.

I see his face, highlighted in the moonlight. I see the winding road, the flash of car headlights. Then I hear the screech of brakes, abrasive and cliched. As I close my eyes now, I hear them again, see the image in front of me. Like an unsettling real-life interpretation of that famous painting, *The Scream*. The thing is, I'm no longer sure if it's an actual memory or something my psyche has constructed over the years. Because if I'm honest, I don't remember seeing his face so clearly. And there was no screech of brakes. There was a shape and a shadow, then a bump. Then nothing. Even at the time, the mundanity of the event sickened me.

But then everything changed, and all I wanted was mundanity.

I shake the thoughts away as the coffee machine chirps and bristles into life. I read somewhere that bad dreams happen when your mind is running through memories of past trauma as a way of better dealing with what happened. I'm not sure about that. But it troubles me why it's suddenly at the forefront of my mind. It feels as if the ghosts of my past are rising from the dead. I thought I'd moved on. I thought I'd pushed those memories – along with who I was back then – so far down inside of me that they wouldn't return. But it seems I was wrong.

Why now?

Why, after twenty years, am I having these dreams again?

I'm not someone who holds much truck with mysticism – tarot cards and crystals and all that crap – but this does seem as if the universe is trying to tell me something. It's a feeling I get. A flutter in the pit of my stomach, a sense of something unattainable to me. It's as if I have the answer, but it's on the cusp of my awareness and I'm only partly aware of it. So I can't grab hold of it or articulate what I'm feeling or thinking into words.

All I know is I want the dreams to stop. I want to never think about what happened. But I can't.

Not until I know for sure that this waking nightmare is over.

For the twentieth time today – the hundredth-plus time in the last few days – I pull my phone out of my pocket and open up the news app. But there's nothing new to read. No new discoveries. No developments. It's been five days now since they found the body. Hopefully, it'll come to nothing, fizzle out like so many cold cases. But who can say?

Even now I feel detached from the story. The memories I hold of that time are like a dim remembrance of a film I once saw; I can't remember the plot or who the actors were. It's a defence mechanism, I suppose. And one that has worked well for me over the years. I might be the most stressed I've ever been and fear any minute the world will open up or the sky will crack and reveal the truth. But, weirdly, I can cope. I can live my life. What that says about me, I don't know. Either I'm very good at disassociating myself from what happened or I'm an evil prick with no soul.

I'm not sure which is worse.

I just want it all to be over. I want none of this to have ever happened. In fact, I've wished for that so much over the last twenty years it's almost as if I've made it true. On a good day, I can kid myself that it didn't happen. Most days it didn't. I was a different person back then. An older, worse version of Rob was there that night. Not me. Not this guy.

Yet, it seems everything comes back around, eventually.

"Evening, Chef."

I look up as Simone leans over the counter. I didn't hear her come in.

"Oh. Hey there. Just in time."

She frowns and looks me up and down. "Are you okay, Rob? You look a bit peaky."

I like Simone. She took over from Jessie as front-of-house last year and has taken to it well. She's great with the customers and helps keep the kitchen running to order – managing my stress levels and shouldering a lot of the minor issues the same way Jessie did. She was born here in Glossop, same as me, but never left, and there's something in her no-nonsense *I speak my mind* attitude that is both refreshing and very much needed in this industry.

"I've not been sleeping well," I tell her. "But I'm fine."

She nods but doesn't look convinced.

"We've got a full house tonight," she says. "That's good, isn't it? First time in a while."

I smile. "Great stuff. Thanks, Simone."

She's about to head through into the kitchen where

the door to the staff room is located but stops in the doorway. "Oh, by the way. Did your mate catch up with you?"

"Yeah," I say, automatically, before realising I've no idea what she's talking about. "Sorry. No. I mean... What mate?"

She pulls a face like I'm crazy.

C'mon, Rob. Get it together.

"Bugger. I didn't get his name. Big guy, with weird hair. A bit scruffy but nice enough. He said he knew you from way back."

The usual fluttering feeling in my stomach makes itself known. "From way back?"

"Yeah. He was in at lunchtime, but I think he just had a coffee." She raises her eyebrows. "Paid with a handful of loose change from what I remember. But it was Carol who dealt with him. She'll know more."

Carol. She's not in yet. But she will be. "Thanks," I tell Simone, then busy myself making a coffee while she hurries away to get herself ready for service.

A mate? From way back? I don't have any mates from way back. None apart from *him*, anyway. But surely it can't be him. The last I heard, he was living down in Brighton. The fluttering grows worse and morphs into a muted feeling of nausea.

It seems too much of a coincidence that he'd appear now. But if he's seen the news, why would he return? It doesn't make sense.

Unless... No!

I can't afford to think that way.

He wouldn't.

He couldn't.

No, it won't be him. I do have other friends. I did, at least. Not that I can recall any of them now, but that's me all over. I don't think about the past. My life started when I met Jessie. Year zero. That's the way it's always been. The way I like it.

So why can't I shake the unpleasant sensation that my world is about to crumble to dust?

This is not what I need right now. Even if it's not him, I don't need the extra stress. Not with everything else – the new baby, the restaurant being on its knees financially, not being able to even talk to my wife about any of it. And on top of all this, she's having a hard time coping with Noah and I feel guilty as hell that I'm not there to support her. I wish she was still here, running front-of-house. At least the restaurant would be less of a stress. She had a way of easing my anxiety and keeping me focused on what was important, on the things I had control over. But that's as good as wishing that what happened twenty years ago hadn't happened.

Is this what karma looks like?

Even if I don't believe in such things, it certainly feels like something ominously serendipitous is going on. The stars are aligning but in the worst possible way. The perfect storm, as they say. Only, it's the lack of any storms that has caused all this shit in the first place.

Global fucking warming.

"Evening, boss." I look up, and a cold shiver runs down my back as I see Carol walking towards me.

"There you are," I say, placing my unused coffee cup in the sink. No time for one now, anyway. "I hear you met a friend of mine today. He was in the restaurant at lunchtime?"

Her mouth turns down as if she doesn't know what I'm talking about and my heart flips over. Thank God. Simone was mistaken. Maybe it was an old friend of Pearl's or another of the kitchen staff.

But then Carol's eyes flash into life and she raises a finger. "Shoot, yeah, sorry. I almost forgot. He was here about one-ish but only had a pot of green tea. I was going to come and get you, but you were really busy in the kitchen, and he said not to bother you." She grimaces. "Sorry, Rob. It was a busy service and after I needed to get off quickly and do a few errands... He did say he'd catch up with you later."

"It's fine," I say, holding out my hand and laughing in the way people do when something really isn't that fine. But it's not the fact she's forgotten to tell me that has me unsettled.

"Who was he? Do you remember his name?"

She looks up to the left, summoning her recall. I don't breathe. Time slows to a stop.

Please don't say it, I think to myself. Please don't say that name. Don't say Dan. Don't say Danny. Don't say Chappers or Chaps or any variant of the name Daniel Chapman at all. That's the last name I want to hear right now. His presence in town makes things real. And it terrifies me. Because if it is him, I know why he's here and what that means for me.

Carol's face relaxes. She flicks her eyebrows as if preparing to reveal a great secret. If only she knew.

"I remember," she says proudly, with a grin. "He was called Dan."

Two days earlier...

Have kids, they said. It would be fun, they said. It's

Sunday, my first day off in over a week, and after a demanding service last night I had – perhaps foolishly – hoped I might have a relaxing day of it. However, right now, I'm engaged in a battle of wills with the immovable force that is my four-year-old daughter.

Fern stares up at me with a cartoonish scowl creasing her little face. It would be cute – nigh on adorable – if I hadn't spent the last ten minutes trying to convince her that scrambled eggs are, in fact, incredibly tasty.

"But, sweetie, you liked them last time you had them," I tell her. "Try them. Go on. Have one mouthful, at least."

"I don't like them. They're all slimy."

"They're creamy. That's how you liked them before. These are proper chef-style scrambled eggs, shorty. The good stuff. I remember last time you told me they were *beautiful.*"

Beautiful is a buzz term in our household at the moment. It's Fern's favourite phrase and she'll apply it to most things. Sunshine, puddles, her Lego creations, the way the toilet block cascades blue residue down the side of the bowl when you flush it. It's very cute. Normally.

"Please. One bite."

"No."

It's hard to argue with her. I find her contrariness rather sweet. And I love that she knows her own mind. It's important. I hope she stays that way.

"Fine." I place the fork down next to her plate. "Why don't we give it a few more minutes and see if you change your mind?"

"I won't."

"Let's see, hey?"

Upstairs, Noah is screaming his little lungs out. The floorboards above us creak as Jessie paces up and down with him in our bedroom. I wonder if I should go up and help out but decide against it. Fern is going through a weird phase right now where she doesn't want to be left alone in the house even for one minute. So, it would mean all of us up in one room on top of each other, each stressing the others out. Times are hard right now in the Wilkes household, but we'll get through it. We have done before.

Have kids, they said. It would be fun, they said.

I know I shouldn't think that way. And I don't. Not really. Except for those moments when I'm desperately clinging to cynicism to remain sane. Our kids are great. Both of them. We're very lucky to have them. For a long time, we thought we wouldn't have any, and that was a trying time for both of us, too. Jessie had three miscarriages before the doctor told her that her womb was 'inhospitable'. What a word to use. Meaning, unwelcoming. Unfriendly. She would have been the most welcoming and friendly mother in the entire world to all three of those babies.

After the third time, I said we should stop trying. It was too painful and neither of us was coping well. Looking back on that time now, I suspect Jessie was actually medically unwell. She cried a lot. When she wasn't crying, I'd find her staring at the wall, staring at nothing. I suggested we see a doctor, but she didn't want to. She didn't want to take pills because she didn't want to stop trying for a baby. So that's what we did. We moved up north, and after two months she got pregnant again. This time, she carried it to full term. Almost. Fern arrived two months premature, and that was a scary time as well. Seeing this tiny little person struggling to breathe in a plastic box every day almost wiped us out. But she was a tough little thing and she got through it. Now she's as robust and cheeky – and as hard work and as *beautiful* – as any four-year-old and we wouldn't have her any other way.

After Fern came home, I felt settled, perhaps for the first time in my adult life. We were certain we wouldn't be able to conceive again and discussed the option of me having a vasectomy. I had no qualms about it like some men do and had even booked myself in for the procedure. But then the first lockdown hit and the world went topsy-turvy and they cancelled my appointment.

Even then, we didn't give it much thought. We had our little miracle to focus on. Fern Edith Wilkes. Our rainbow baby. She was more than enough. But then last December Jessie started being sick and we found out she was expecting again. It was a complete surprise, but I don't think either of us allowed ourselves to even consider the possibility she'd go full term. We waited, living day to day, until eight months and twenty-one days rolled around, and Noah was born. That was three weeks ago. I don't think I've fully come to terms with his arrival yet, and I think Jessie is the same. We're both in shock. But in a good way. I think. The truth is neither of us has had a second's peace or time to catch our breaths for so long that I'm not even sure what I think about anything anymore.

Footsteps on the stairs have me turning from the table. Jessie is standing in the doorway with a face like thunder and eyes like rain clouds. I smile at her but she holds her hand up to me as if I'll set her off if I say anything.

"He's asleep," she whispers. "Finally."

"Good work. Sorry. I didn't know whether to come up or not."

She blows out a breath and it appears to calm her. "It's

fine. I knew you were busy with this one." She walks over and leans over Fern's chair. "Are you not eating Daddy's lovely eggs, Ferny?"

"They're slimy, apparently," I tell her, raising my eyebrows.

Jessie sticks out her bottom lip in solidarity. "I'm sure they're not." She takes Fern's pink-handled fork and scoops a mound of eggs into her mouth. "Mmm, delicious. You're missing out, kiddo."

"I don't like them," Fern says.

"Fair enough."

Jessie places the fork down and walks over to the fridge. She opens it and stares inside.

"What are you looking for?" I ask.

"I'm not sure." She closes it again and walks to the sink. She looks worn out.

"Noah still running you ragged?"

She nods. "I don't know what to do. I feel as if he hates me. Most of the time he won't settle unless he's completely knackered himself out from screaming."

I walk over to her, so we can talk seriously out of earshot of Fern. "You're doing great, Jess. And of course he doesn't hate you. He loves you. Like we all do." I place my hand on her cheek and she leans into it, closing her eyes.

"I just wish you had more time at home to help out," she says before opening her eyes and adding, "But I get you have to work. I know how important it is to have you onsite in the restaurant now we're back to full capacity and doing lunchtimes as well."

She says it like she's read my script. I glance at Fern, but she's engrossed in playing with her scrambled eggs and forking them into what passes as a half-decent flower shape.

"It won't be for too much longer," I say.

"Really? So, it's all going to plan?"

"Yeah. Everything is going well."

She frowns. "You don't sound very convincing, babe."

"The restaurant is fine," I tell her.

"Is Simone still running front-of-house?"

"Yep. She's doing well." I move back to the table and sit. "But she's no Jessie Wilkes. You're still missed by all the staff."

"I'm not sure about that. But thanks."

Our eyes meet and I give her what I hope is a reassuring smile.

She glances around. "Are there any eggs for me?

Bugger. I should have made more.

I didn't think.

"I can put some more on. Do you want me to?"

"Please. I'm starving."

She gets herself a glass of water and sits opposite Fern whilst I rescue my favourite pan from the dishwasher and give it a wash. As I crack some eggs into a bowl, I wait for Jessie to say something to Fern, but she doesn't. When I turn around, she's staring out the window. She looks tired. She looks like I feel.

I've only had a slice of toast so I make enough eggs for both of us and a fresh pot of coffee. After setting Fern up with a new mermaid colouring book we eat in relative silence, the air punctuated only by Fern's squeaky voice, informing us what colour she's doing each section of the picture and asking us to look at how beautiful her colouring-in is.

"That's amazing," I tell her. "You're so good at staying in the lines these days. Excellent work." She is a great colourer, but I also try to give her plenty of praise whenever I can do. I want my daughter to grow up to be a strong, confident person. Someone who can stand up for herself and who trusts herself to make the right decisions when it counts. That's very important.

As I'm watching her I sense Jessie watching me and glance over to her.

"What's going on, babe?" she asks.

The question blindsides me. "What do you mean?"

"You seem distracted at the moment. I don't feel like we've connected properly in ages. Since before Noah was born."

I want to tell her it's her who's distracted. And that I'd even go so far as to say distant at times. It's a bit of a head-screwer. One minute she can be nice as pie, bright and caring and fun to be around – the Jessie I fell in love with – and the next minute she's in a dark mood but won't tell me what's bothering her. I know life as a new mum is tough and she's doing the best she can but not knowing which version of her I'm going to get from one moment to the next only adds to my stress levels.

"I'm fine," I say. "Are you?"

"Is there anything you want to tell me?"

"Like what?"

She raises her eyebrows in a gesture full of subtext. The same with the way she runs her tongue slowly across her teeth. As usual, I can't work out what she's getting at. But she might say that's the problem.

"So, Fire and Ice – our only source of income – is doing well? Because last time I looked at the books, they didn't look so great."

A prickly heat spreads across my chest and up my neck. "I've just told you. It's fine. Don't worry. Everything is going well." I don't mean to snap, but I can't help it.

"Are you keeping something from me, Rob? Because you know I hate secrets. Remember what we said, what you promised me."

I do remember. And I know I should be honest with her. But right now, this is my burden and my problem to sort out. She's got enough on with Noah and getting her strength back after the birth. Noah was a healthy baby, but it was a tricky labour and Jessie lost a lot of blood. She still looks weak and pale. I don't like keeping things from her. Not after everything we've said to each other, but it's for the best. This is my problem to sort out.

"Everything is good," I say, but as I meet her gaze, I notice how bloodshot her eyes are.

What a self-centred prick I am.

We've been here together talking and eating for at least thirty minutes and it's the first time I've properly noticed her. It says a lot about our current situation.

"Are you sure you're okay?" I ask. "You look like you've been crying."

She shrugs it off. "It's an emotional time."

I smile. "Do you want another coffee?" As I ask, the sound of crying emanates down the stairs. I grimace. "Do you want me to go?"

"No," she says, pushing off from the table and getting to her feet. "He'll want me. Or, more specifically, he'll want boob. He's just take, take, take, this guy. Like all men."

I laugh, but as she leaves the room and heads upstairs, a sinking feeling in my stomach tells me it probably wasn't a joke.

2

I'm sitting in the front room later that night, sipping at a cup of camomile tea, when Jessie enters carrying a large glass of white wine.

"Having a drink?" I say it without thinking, but as soon as the words have left my mouth, I regret it.

She slumps in the chair next to the sofa where I'm sprawled. "I'm only having the one. I think I've earned it."

I push myself upright, so I don't look like so much of a slob. "Yes, of course. One glass. Go for it." She's still breast-feeding, so it's not advisable to drink too much alcohol. But I've read the literature and all the stuff on Mumsnet and similar forums. I know one glass is acceptable. Perhaps a smaller glass than the one she's poured herself, but I'd rather not argue about it.

"Hopefully now he'll sleep through until – ooo... maybe two-ish," she adds, taking a large gulp. "What joy. I might get a few unbroken hours' sleep if I'm lucky."

I sit all the way up. "What's that supposed to mean?"

She huffs. "Nothing. Sorry. Ignore me."

"I'll get up with him if you want. But last time I offered you said—"

"It's fine. Really," she says, with a smile. "I've just got a lot going on, Rob. Hormones. You know how I can get. You've got a lot on too, I know that."

I watch her for a few more seconds, hoping she'll look at me so I can let her know with my reasoned facial expressions that I understand. But she doesn't.

I turn my attention to the television. I was half-watching an old episode of *Homes Under The Hammer*, but it's finished, so I flick through the channels, landing on the local news.

"Leave this on," Jessie says. So I do.

On-screen, a man in a wax jacket is talking to someone holding a large kestrel that keeps trying to fly away but is snared by a piece of leather attached to the keeper's glove. It's typical local news fair and I quickly zone out, my mind drifting to more solemn and pressing matters. I really should sit down with Jessie and discuss our finances. But, then, there are a lot of things I should discuss with Jessie. Every morning I wake up and I have so many ideas about what I'm going to do that day, things I'm going to sort out, things I'm going to make right. I'm sure she's the same. But by the evening we're both so exhausted and our sensibilities so fried, all we want to do is eat dinner and veg out in front of the television.

I watch her as she watches the news. Even with no sleep and not yet back to her full health, she's still the same attractive – *beautiful* – girl I fell in love with ten years ago. She's a good person is Jessie. Loyal, funny, wise. She's been an excellent foil for me over the years, and I don't know what the hell I'd do without her. I certainly don't know where I'd be now if we'd never met. I might be living in London still. I might have made it bigger in the industry.

I might also be dead.

"Have you seen this?" she says, gesturing at the screen. "It's crazy."

I turn to look at the television in time to see a drone shot of what I can instantly see is Woodhead Reservoir, just down the road from our house. Only, it's almost devoid of water. As the camera pans across the scene, it shows small pools separated by vast areas of bare earth. In some places, the grass is even starting to grow.

"Whoa," I say, as a ripple of nervous energy runs down my back. "It's almost dried up."

Jessie tuts. "It's going to happen more and more though, isn't it? We're in the middle of a full-on climate crisis. Just to add to every other bleeding crisis we've got going on!"

I hear her, but I don't answer. I can't take my eyes off the screen. "Can you turn it up?" I ask. "I can't hear what they're talking about."

"You've got the buttons."

I scrabble around my person for the remote control and find it stuffed down the back of the cushion. As I turn up the volume, I catch the last of the report. The voiceover is saying how water levels have been rapidly sinking all summer and are still on the decline.

"Recent heatwaves, with temperatures soaring to over thirty degrees Celsius in parts of Derbyshire, have left the region's reservoirs at low capacity. In the most recent figures, published on their website, water levels at Woodhead Reservoir were at just twenty-nine percent. We can compare this to an average of seventy-six percent the previous year."

The reporter finishes by saying, in an exasperated

tone, that we should expect hosepipe bans but that High Peak Council have yet to issue any restrictions. I allow myself to breathe again. It's a fluff piece. Nothing to worry about.

But as the report ends with a lingering shot of the dried-up reservoir, a feeling of dread blossoms inside of me. Another week of hot weather and the water in the reservoir could be completely gone. What then? If all the water disappears, there's a chance that...

No!

I shake the thought away.

Don't think about it.

I switch the television off.

"Hey! I was watching that."

I look at Jessie. "It was finished. And it was a nothing story, anyway. It'll rain soon enough and fill up again. These things happen."

"Do they? I've never seen a reservoir dried up like that. Not in this country. Not in Derbyshire." She takes another large gulp of wine and catches me looking. "For heaven's sake, Rob. Can you not?"

"What am I doing?"

"Looking at me like I'm injecting cocaine into my eyeballs or something. It's one glass of wine."

"It's a large glass."

She glares at me. "Oh, I see. So, you are being prissy about it?"

"I'm not."

I wasn't.

What I'm probably doing is trying to distract myself from the torment of dark thoughts swirling in my head. But even being aware of that doesn't shut me up.

"If you think it's fine, it's fine."

"Yes, I do think it's fine. Thank you. I'm honest about what I do. Unlike some people."

I place my cup of tea on the small table next to the sofa. Here we go again. It seems whatever we talk about these days, it returns to something along these lines. After six years of marriage and two kids, she still doesn't trust that I love her and I'm not going to cheat on her. It can be so draining at times.

"I'm always honest with you, Jessie. No secrets. We agreed."

"Yes, *we* did. But I know there are things you aren't telling me. I'm not stupid, Rob. I can tell when you're keeping things from me."

"For fuck's sake, Jessie. I'm not keeping anything from you." My voice has inadvertently risen a couple of octaves. It doesn't make me sound convincing.

The problem is, I know why Jessie is like this, and I am partly to blame. When I was younger, before we met, I was a bit of a hellraiser, truth be told. Not in the booze and drugs sense – I've been teetotal since my twenties – but I partied a lot. I slept with a lot of women. With hindsight, I suspect it was a cry for help – me trying to lose myself in other people, a way of dealing with what happened by expending my energy and focus elsewhere. But I couldn't tell Jessie that. Explaining it would bring up more questions than I could answer.

So, I kept quiet about my past. I didn't tell her who I really was. Or, rather, who I'd been. Telling someone how many people you've slept with isn't advisable on a first date anyway, especially when that total is over three digits – and as our relationship blossomed, the right time to reveal my lothario past never came up. Added to this, Jessie had already confided in me that her last two boyfriends had cheated on her and turned out to be total players. I didn't want her to mark me down as being the same.

But of course, she found out. People always do. We were down in London, at my cousin Jonathan's wedding, when a drunk girl stormed up to us and informed Jessie that I was a total bastard and that I'd ghosted her. She went on to explain that she knew of at least three other girls to whom I'd done the same thing. After that, it all came out. Most of it, at least. Jessie was mortified I'd never told her. She said it was a betrayal of trust.

"So, what is it, Rob? Is it the restaurant? Or something else?"

"No! The restaurant is doing fine."

"So, it's something else? Some*one* else? Is that it? You think I'm unattractive. But why wouldn't you? Well, I'm sorry, but I've just had a child ripped out of me!" She bursts into tears. I instinctively leap up and go to her but she turns away. "No. Please don't. I can't take it. I'm so sorry, Rob. I don't know what's going on with me right now. I feel as if I've no control over myself."

"Jess. You've nothing to worry about. I swear to you. I don't think any of those things! I think you're beautiful! You are beautiful! Like always."

Bloody hell.

Why can't we just have a quiet evening without a lot of stress and upset?

I really need a quiet evening.

"I know there's something, Rob. It's written all over your face. You've gone white."

"Have I?"

"Yes," she pleads, tears rolling down her face. "What is it?"

"Nothing. I swear to you."

She wipes at her face with her sleeve. "Okay. Fine. I'm going to bed." She gets up off the chair and I'm relieved. I've got a lot of shit in my head right now and I need time to process it. To work out what I'm going to do if the worst thing happens.

Jessie shuffles over to the door but stops and turns back to me. When she speaks her voice is quiet and wavering. "You said no more secrets. You told me that. You promised."

"And I meant it," I say. "I still do. If I had something – anything – important to tell you, I would. But there's nothing wrong. You don't have anything to worry about, I promise. Please don't do this, Jess. Me and you are great. Everything is great." I hold her gaze and smile, willing her with all I've got to believe me.

She narrows her eyes for a second and then nods. "Right. I'm going to bed."

"Okay. I'll be up soon. I love you."

"I love you too," she whispers. Then she disappears around the corner. I listen for her footsteps on the stairs before sitting back and letting out a long sigh. It's as if I've released a whole lifetime of emotion, but it doesn't seem to do any good. I still feel tense and I'm struggling to focus on any one thought in particular.

Grabbing up the remote control, I switch the television back on and mute it as I flick through the channels to see if there are any other news stories about Woodhead Reservoir. There aren't any. I switch the television off and carry my mug and Jessie's empty wine glass through into the kitchen. As I enter, I see the bottle of wine on the kitchen table. It's half full and still cold as I pick it up. A Chablis. One of the ones from Jaspers Wine

Merchants, our suppliers at the restaurant. It's good stuff, so I'm told.

I place Jessie's empty glass next to the bottle and screw off the top. It smells good. Heady and dangerous and full of adventure. Like the old days. I haven't drunk since that day twenty years ago, but one glass wouldn't hurt, would it? It's not like I have a problem. I don't think so, at least. It might help me sleep tonight.

I hold onto the stem of the wine glass and lower the neck of the bottle over the rim. It hovers there for a moment before I place the bottle back on the table.

Don't be stupid.

I screw the top back on and walk the bottle over to the fridge before I change my mind. One thing I know to be true: you don't solve one problem by creating another. No matter how tempting it might be. I place the bottle in the fridge and the glass and my mug in the sink and turn out the light.

As I walk back into the front room, I can hear Jessie finishing up in the bathroom. I hear the click of the light and her walking down the corridor to our room. If I go up now, by the time I've cleaned my teeth and got ready for bed she'll be asleep. No more talking. No more arguing or accusations.

I feel awful about keeping things from her. Or, heaven forbid, gaslighting her. Because she's right. I did promise her.

"No more secrets," I whisper to myself.

I will talk to her about the restaurant soon enough. Just as soon as the finances are a bit less dire. I'll tell her everything. Like a good husband should do.

No more secrets.

Except for the one I can't ever tell anyone about.

3

ire and Ice doesn't open until the evening on
Mondays but that doesn't mean I can afford to
take time off in the daytime. There are dishes to
prep, contractors to meet with, receipts and invoices to
check. Today I'm driving over to Holmfirth to meet with
Barry Biggins, a young farmer and a supplier of organic
local pork.

My house stands on its own land just outside of
Glossop town centre. So, I'm only in the van for five
minutes, driving along Woodhead Road, before I get eyes
on the reservoirs up ahead. They already look more dried-
up than they did on last night's news report. There are
vast areas with no water at all. Just dry mud and grass. As I
get closer, I turn down the radio – as if somehow that will
help me concentrate. Or deal with what I'm about to see.

It's only a few minutes after ten but the sun is already
baking hot through the windscreen and there are no
clouds in the sky. It's going to be another scorcher.

At some point, Woodhead Road turns into the A628.
I'm never sure exactly where, even after all these years,

and this A-road winds through the valley, alongside three reservoirs and through the Peak District National Park towards West Yorkshire and the road to Sheffield. There are actually four reservoirs in this area. Valeside, Rhodeswood, Torside and then the largest one, Woodhead. They're laid out in a line with the A628 passing alongside each one. As I drive on, I see they're all as barren as each other. But it's Woodhead that's the main concern. It's the biggest one. The one most people think about if they think about reservoirs in the area. It's certainly the one I think about. The one I see in my dreams.

And now the water is all but gone. Dried-up. Ready to reveal its murky depths and its secrets to the world. But, surely after all these years, there is nothing to be found down there but mud and rock. That's what I tell myself, at least, as I drive on past the turn-off for the A6024. This is the road to Holmfirth and will deliver me straight to Barry's farm in no time at all. But I don't turn off. I never turn off. The A6024 is winding and steep and can be treacherous in bad weather, but that's not the reason why I avoid that route. The story I like to tell myself is that sticking to the A628 is better in the long run. I can still get to Barry this way and it's a less stressful drive. The story I like to tell myself is I prefer it this way.

Barry is waiting at the gate of his drive as I emerge around the last bend on the dirt track that leads to his farm.

"I thought you weren't coming," he bellows, as I wind the window down to greet him.

Despite being younger than me and his website describing him as an *Artisan Butcher,* Barry is a typical

Yorkshire farmer. Red-cheeked and rotund in figure. Jolly and brusque in equal measure.

"Sorry, I got a bit waylaid," I tell him. But I'm only a few minutes late. "Are you getting in?"

"Nah, I'll meet you over there."

I drive the van slowly around the side of the first building, keeping Barry in my rear-view mirror as I go. I bring the van to a stop next to the outbuilding where he keeps his produce and where he's got a small dining area set up along one wall.

It's here where we sit to do business and, once I'm settled, Barry disappears through a door over on one side of the room, appearing a few minutes later with a large platter of meat.

"This is the best belly pork you're ever gonna put in ya mouth," he says, placing the plate down in front of me. On it are four different versions of his prized produce, fatty and unctuous and cut into perfect squares. From first perusal, I'd say I'm trying regular and wood-smoked versions and two which have been marinated. One in a violent red mix that smells strongly of paprika and the other in oil, peppercorns and herbs.

"Go on, lad," Barry says. "Get stuck in."

And I do. Despite it only being late morning, I've not eaten breakfast and the salty meat tastes delicious. I quickly scoff down one of each portion. The fat is perfectly rendered down with crispy skin and each morsel is a sublime journey of flavour and texture.

"This is wonderful," I tell Barry. "I think I'd definitely like some of the wood-smoked. I've got a dish I'm developing that it'd be perfect for."

"Good stuff." Barry sits down finally and cracks his

knuckles. "Now I should tell ya – prices have risen a touch since you were last here, Robert."

"I see." I smile and shrug but presumably can't hide the bitter undercurrent to this gesture as Barry puffs out his cheeks at me.

"Sorry about that. You know how it is, mate. Times are tricky right now. And for everyone, I do know that."

Do you, mate?

You own about a hundred acres of land. You might not be cash rich, but you'll never be homeless.

I keep my smile on regardless, allowing these unhelpful thoughts to fade as I take another piece of wood-smoked belly pork from the plate. It's not helpful to be bitter. And Barry is right. We are all struggling right now in the food industry. You can blame Brexit, or the cost-of-living crisis, or the war in Ukraine all you want but it doesn't help. It doesn't put bums on seats. I have to remain optimistic.

It's important to only focus on things you do have control over.

Although, it's hard. Since last night, the dried-up reservoir has never been far from my thoughts, and as Barry goes off on one of his truncated monologues about his pigs and the pork industry, I'm there again on the bridge, gazing into the dark water below. As he talks I make the right noises, nod and grimace at the right times, but I can't concentrate. Just driving along that road today, it brought up so much negative energy. I felt it physically.

It's weird; for a long time I managed to keep what happened that night out of my thoughts. When Jessie and I got together I was madly in love and all my attention was on her. Then we had all the pain and heartache of the miscarriages. Even when we moved back here, we were focusing all our energy, all our thoughts and dreams, on getting pregnant. Then, when our little miracle came along, it was Fern that occupied my mind twenty-four seven. I even allowed myself to feel happy. Content, even.

What a bloody idiot.

Talk about tempting fate.

All at once it feels as if the world is trying to suffocate me. I've got a business in crisis, a wife who doesn't trust me, and a tiny baby whom I've yet to bond with. Add to that the bad dreams. The sleepless nights. The paranoia. The torment.

It's a wonder I'm still able to operate.

Whoa, Jesus.

I almost had the thought just then – *why me?* As if I didn't deserve any of this. But I do. Even if I'm incredibly skilled at telling myself otherwise.

Old habits die hard.

And being this way is how I am still able to operate. It's how I get through each day without going crazy from shame and torment. I tell myself that it wasn't me back then, it wasn't who I am today. I tell myself the modern version of Rob Wilkes would not make those same decisions. He would admit what he'd done.

The only problem is, if I'm honest with myself, I can't say for certain that any of that is true.

And what does that say about me?

That I'm good at deflecting blame?

That I'm a psychopath?

That I'm evil?

Or that I'm such a coward I still can't face up to what I did. It's head in the sand all the way for good old Robby. I've been running away from my problems all my life.

Only, there comes a time when you run out of road.

4

I buy twelve packs of wood-smoked pork belly from Barry and he convinces me to take another four packs of the herb-infused stuff as well. I have an idea for a small plate that would go down well at the Spanish night I'm planning next month. We try to put a theme night on every so often, and they're always popular. Three courses with amuse-bouche on entry and coffee and petit fours to finish. We don't make much profit on these nights – in fact, we almost run at a loss – but it's good to see the place sold out and it helps promote the business.

Once the van is loaded up, Barry slaps the roof with his big hand and I reverse down the dirt track towards the road, turning around in the first passing point I come across. The old analogue clock on the dashboard reads 12 noon. which means it's actually 1 p.m. I never got around to changing it when the clocks went forward. My plan is to take the pork over to the restaurant and have a twenty-minute snooze in the back room before heading home. I know it's selfish of me to not go straight back and help

Jessie with Noah, but I need some rest if I'm going to make it through service this evening. Plus, after a decent power nap, I'll be refreshed and clear-minded enough to help out with the kids before work.

With all this on my mind, I've taken the first left out of the farm and am driving down the A6024 before I realise what I've done. When I snap back into the present I put my foot on the brake immediately and slow to a stop. There are no other cars around and my first thought is to do a U-turn and go back the way I've come. But time is pressing on. I have driven along this road on a handful of occasions in the last twenty years and it's not as if I'm likely to freak out or anything like that. Yet, what concerns me is how much coincidence seems to be playing a part in my life right now. It does feel as if the universe is holding up a mirror to my past, determined for me to come to terms with what happened.

But, why?

And why now?

Another thought comes to mind. A phrase I read in one of the many self-help books I consumed once I'd hit rock bottom and realised I had to turn my life around.

What you resist persists.

Meaning, if you don't deal with your problems, they keep coming back. The fact that this old phrase has popped into my head feels pertinent. Is it possible that all this stress – the dreams, the memories bubbling up inside of me – is actually my subconscious letting me know I should finally face things and move on? It's also possible I'm deflecting, telling myself a version of the story that keeps me as the main character. The good guy. Because that's who I am. I am a good guy. Even good guys make mistakes sometimes.

I shove the van into first gear and set off again. I can do this. It's just a strip of tarmac and dirt. It doesn't mean anything.

I turn on the radio. The song playing is an old Elton John number and I'm not a huge fan but I turn the volume up until the van's small speakers start to distort and buzz. This way the music fills my head rather than any dark memories.

Or so I hope.

As I get to the bend where the road crosses Withens Brook I find myself slowing down. I bring the van to a stop just around the bend, right where it happened. Rather than turn off the engine, I put the stick into neutral and open the driver's door. I don't know why I keep the engine idling, maybe in case I need to make a quick getaway. The sun is right above me and, along with the blue sky and lush green fields on either side, the scene feels far too incongruent as I step out onto the roadside. I sense an outside force guiding me as I walk over to the dry-stone wall at the side of the road and look out over the valley. It's a hot day but a shiver runs down my body regardless as I take in the barren reservoir.

Standing here now, I realise it's almost twenty years ago, to the day, that it happened. I was eighteen and it was late summer. Dan and I had just finished our A-Levels. It was supposed to be a time of freedom and adventure. It was, in a way. But not in the way I expected.

I suck in a deep breath and hold it in my lungs. Good air quality, that's what you get in the countryside. It's crisp and fresh and full of oxygen. As I take in more breaths, my mind wanders once more into the past. The air up here was one reason why Jessie wanted to move here after the third miscarriage. My dad still lives over in Hadfield, and

Jessie and I would come up and visit him regularly. Each time, she'd mention how lovely the area was and how healthy she felt when she was away from the hustle and bustle of London. Her idea was that it would be beneficial to be somewhere out in the open, away from the pollutants and toxicity of the big city. Back then I would have done anything to make her happy. I still would. But whether it was a good idea, I'm not sure. Not when the past feels so close. Still, two healthy kids later, she might have been onto something.

It's strange. Being here, on the exact bit of road where it happened twenty years earlier, I still don't feel what I think I should feel. There's the usual torment and anguish – and now you can add dread and paranoia to that mix – but guilt? I don't know. I feel something. Shame, perhaps. Sorrow, too – for him and any family he left behind. But I can feel all those without putting myself into the equation. I don't know if it's a self-defence mechanism or me being a cold-blooded psychopath, but often I find that the more horrible an experience the more I feel detached from it. It's like I'm living in the world once removed from my life. I look around me and see what's actually there but don't feel either good or bad about it. I just feel apart. I read the awful news reports on social media. I see the harrowing images on television, but I don't let anything register too deeply. I like to tell myself it's because I used to be too sensitive and being that way almost destroyed me, so since then I've built a wall of protection around my heart. But I don't know if that's true.

What I kept telling myself in the years after the accident was that the poor man was already dead. We couldn't change that. If we'd called the police, we'd have ruined both our lives as well as his. It was an awful accident. A terrible tragedy. Wiping out two more lives over one stupid mistake didn't seem fair. We fucked up, I know that. But destroying our chances of a decent future wasn't going to bring the poor bastard back to life.

That's the dichotomy of being me, I suppose. I know I did something unforgivable, but I can't say for sure I wouldn't do the same thing if it happened today. Because you have to protect yourself. And now I have to protect those I love as well. That's life. That's human nature.

I close my eyes and draw back another lungful of air. The sun is warm on my cheeks. It feels good. I'm alive. I'm not a bad person.

My eyes snap open as I hear something off in the distance. At first, I think it's a pneumatic drill but as I listen the sound becomes more distinct, and I realise it's a helicopter. From the sound of it, it's coming this way.

My fleeting moment of contentment turns to trepidation and then to cold fear as I hear another sound piercing the air. The whirring siren of a police car. In fact, it sounds as if there's more than one.

I rush back to the van and clamber in behind the wheel, grinding the stick into first gear. I check my mirrors, check my blind spot. I can't see the police cars or the helicopter but that doesn't mean they aren't close. I pull away from the roadside and drive back to the restaurant as fast as my nerves and the speed limit allow.

PEARL LEANS over the chrome countertop so she can make eye contact with me. "Are you sure you're all right, Chef?"

I screw my eyes up, pinching the top of my nose at the same time. "Yes. Sorry, mate. I'm just knackered. I wanted to have a nap in the backroom before service, but I couldn't get off." Even as I say the words the guilt hits me like a fist in the guts. I shouldn't even be here. Not yet. After my failed attempt at sleep, I should have gone home and helped Jessie with the kids. But when things get on top of me, I need positive distractions more than I need air. So, I stayed here and put all my attention on inventing a new dish.

I open my eyes wide to focus on the plate in front of me. Off-centre on the plate is a piece of Barry's wood-smoked pork belly that I've rubbed with aromatic spices before cooking sous vide and then finishing in the pan for maximum flavour. Delicate domes of apple and celeriac puree, candied hazelnuts, and soy-glazed sprouting broccoli accompany the protein along with a glorious red wine jus – if I do say so myself.

"It looks and smells fantastic," Pearl says, reaching across me for a knife and fork. "Can I try it?"

"Absolutely. Go for it." I step back so I can watch her reaction. She cuts off a bit of the pork belly and scoops up a little of each puree before placing the fork gingerly into her mouth.

"Mmm. Good," she says, nodding and holding her hand over her mouth. "The meat is amazing. So tender."

"Yeah, but it's missing something," I tell her. "I can't work out what."

"Nah, it's delicious. And you always say it needs more. You're never happy with anything."

I smile. She has no idea how true that is. "More salt?"

She tilts her head from side to side. "Only a touch. Perhaps we need a bit more sharpness in the sauce."

"There! You see!" I wave my finger at her. "More acid. I like it. That's a great palate you've got there, Pearl."

"Yeah, yeah." She shuffles her shoulders in a little

dance, perhaps to cover any awkwardness. Pearl is a great chef and she's come far. When I met her, she was a troubled kid with no prospects and a bad attitude. She started with us five years ago as a pot washer, when Fire and Ice had just opened. The job centre linked us with her as part of some new initiative, and she made it clear from the start that she didn't want to be here. Yet, over time, I gave her more and more tasks. Chopping veg, making sauces. She picked it up fast and eventually the abrasiveness faded. She started to like the work and I liked teaching her. She was still a little rough around the edges but that didn't bother me. I think she reminded me of myself when I was her age. And she's proved herself ten times over since then. She's going to be one hell of a head chef one day. As I say, I'd love her to take over the reins here; she's almost ready, but it's just not viable yet. Give it six months, a year, for me to get the finances in order, and we'll see.

"Why don't you have a go at it yourself?" I tell her.

"What? Are you serious?"

"Have you done all your prep?" She nods. "Your area wiped down and ready for service?" Another nod. "Right, then. You've got forty minutes before the first covers are in. Show me what you can do with more acid."

She giggles but I can tell she's excited. "Okay. I will."

"Good stuff. Now, where the hell did I put my phone?"

Pearl looks around as I do the dance of patting my pockets to search for it. "I think I saw it by the till in the dining room," she says.

"Yes. Of course. Thanks. What would I do without you!" I pat her on the shoulder and head out into the main space of the restaurant. The lights are still off but I don't turn them on. Instead, I grab my phone, sit down at the nearest table and let out a long, deliberate sigh. I've been sighing like this a lot these last few days. It's supposed to help ease tension. I wish.

On opening up my phone I see I've got two missed calls and a flurry of WhatsApp messages from Jessie. She starts off wanting to know where I am and then gets more and more abusive as it dawns on her I'm not coming home before service.

Good one, mate. Going for Husband of the Year again, are we?

What a wanker.

What a selfish prick.

After all the commotion with the police sirens and helicopters earlier, my heart was pounding when I got back to the restaurant. There was no way I was going to settle down for a nap after that. Even if I had managed to get to sleep, it would have probably made me feel worse. I woke up last night in a cold sweat. It was that dream again. The same one as the night before. The same dream I always have when I wake up in a cold sweat. And that's not me using a cliched saying, either. It's an actual cold, wet clamminess. My t-shirt was stuck to my back and I looked as if I'd been in the shower with it on.

When I was in my twenties, I used to wake up screaming or I'd yell things out in my sleep. Nothing incriminating, thankfully, at least not from what I could gather from those unfortunate women who had chosen to share a bed with me on those particular nights. But I did worry.

The thing is, I thought the dreams had stopped.

They had stopped.

Years ago.

I message Jessie back, telling her how sorry I am and that I got held up at one of the suppliers. It's another half-truth and I feel a prickle of unpleasantness in my body when I hit send, but it's for the best. I don't want to upset her. She's very highly strung right now and anything can tip her over the edge. I make a promise to myself that I'll try to be a better husband and father from now on. But it's hard. I feel like I've got twenty plates spinning all at once and they're about to crash to the ground. I want to spend time with my family, enjoy Fern and Noah when they're still young, and take some of the strain off Jessie, but to do that I need to employ a head chef and I can't afford to. The result is, of course, that no one is happy, and I'm so stressed out I'm probably more of a hindrance in the restaurant than I am a help. But I don't know what else I can do. I have to keep those plates spinning. It's all on me if one of them falls.

I get up and saunter back into the kitchen. Pearl is stirring at a sauce on the stove, her face hard with concentration as she tastes it with a teaspoon. She glances over at me as I enter but doesn't say anything.

Next to her our junior, Lawrence, is feverishly peeling potatoes, and on the other side of him Tony, our chef de partie responsible for deserts, is portioning up one of his signature yuzu and black sesame seed custard tarts. It buoys me to see them all so hard at work, like a finely tuned machine all moving in the same direction. The way a proper kitchen should be.

"Is everyone okay?" I say, lowering my voice to an authoritative tone.

"Yes, Chef!"

"Great. The first covers are due in twenty minutes. Let's have a good service, everyone."

"Yes, Chef!"

I like it when work is like this. There's a spark of energy in the air. It takes me out of myself. My dad always says that busy hands equal a quiet mind and he's certainly not wrong. But then, my old man is rarely wrong about anything and I'm lucky to have him so close. I make another mental note to go and visit him soon. Maybe tomorrow afternoon. Pearl and the team can manage without me for lunch service for once, and I could take Noah with me whilst Fern is at pre-school. It'll give Jessie a few hours on her own. She'll like that. So will my old man. We'll all like it.

Smiling to myself at my quick turnaround in attitude, I head back into the main space and switch on the house lights, ready for the first guests to arrive. As I'm doing so, Simone and Carol both arrive together through the main door at the far side of the restaurant.

"Evening, Rob. Chef," Simone says, with a wink. "Everything good?"

"Yes. Everything is good, thank you. You?"

"Not bad. Yeah."

"Did you see the news?" Carol adds as they both shuffle past me into the kitchen and head for the staff room.

"What news?" I follow them through, an uneasy feeling spreading up through my torso as I go. "What do you mean?"

Carol stops and turns to the room as if addressing the whole team. "They've found a body," she says. "In the reservoir. Apparently, it was lodged under some roots at the bottom but became exposed as the water dried up.

Some man walking his dog saw it from the hillside and called it in. It's only happened in the last few hours. The police are swarming over the area now. It's all cordoned off and the traffic is backed right up through Hadfield. Luckily, I was staying at Geoff's last night or I wouldn't have made it in."

Someone says something else.

Someone gasps.

But I'm not sure. It feels as if the walls are closing in on me. I can't breathe. I can't focus on anything. I worry I'm having a stroke, but this thought only sends me spiralling further into the abyss. I glance around. No one is looking at me. Why aren't they looking at me?

Can't they see I'm dying?

I'm literally about to keel over!

I gulp back air, trying to calm my breathing as I grasp at the edge of the counter to steady myself.

"Do they know who it is?" Pearl asks.

"Not yet," Carol says. "Do you remember Geoff's sister is in the police? She gave us the heads-up. But she's not got much info herself. It's early days. But apparently, it looks to have been in there a long time."

The room clicks back into focus. I glance at the clock above the main stove. Ten minutes until we open.

"All right, everyone," I say, but when no one turns around I realise I've only whispered it. I cough and straighten my back, raising my voice to say, "All right, people. I know this is all very exciting, but can we get to work, please!"

They carry on talking.

"Hey! Can we get back to work, please? We're getting ready to open. Simone, Carol. Can you put your bags in the staff room and start welcoming guests, please?" Now they turn around and Simone gives me a funny look. I ignore her and turn to the others. "Lawrence, is all your prep done?"

"Yes."

"Yes, what?"

"Yes, Chef!"

"Good. Then let's start acting like professionals. Pearl, can you get on the pass for a minute and wipe the counter down, please? I need to make sure I—argh!"

I go to pick up Pearl's saucepan and burn my palm on the handle.

"Shit! Bugger!"

I let go and spill the hot sticky jus all over the stovetop.

"Chef!" Pearl yells. "Come over here."

She puts an arm around my shoulders and guides me over to the two industrial sinks where she twists on the cold tap. "Put it under here, quick, before it blisters."

I do as she says, glad of her presence but feeling as if I'm four years old. The water runs ice cold and numbs the pain in my hand. My palm is red on one side and down the side of my forefinger, but it doesn't look too bad. It was a stupid thing to do. A rookie mistake.

"Are you sure everything's okay with you?" Pearl asks in a lowered voice.

I turn and force a smile. "Yes. Thanks, mate. I'm just a bit stressed right now. About a few things. Personal stuff. Nothing for you to worry about. We'll have a good service, yeah?"

She grins. "Of course we will. Fire and Ice all the way, baby!"

I gesture over to the pass with my chin. "You go and get ready. I'll sort myself from here. Thank you, though."

"No worries." She hurries away and I turn back to the sink, staring at my hand as the water cascades over it.

A body.

They've found a body.

The one thing I've feared more than anything else in my life has happened. Strangely, now that the initial shock is beginning to subside, I don't know how I feel about it. I don't feel as terrified as I imagined I would. It's almost like the worst thing has happened and I'm still standing. I'm coping. Just about, at least. I've no idea what's going to happen next, but I've got to try to keep it together. The ghosts of my past have finally risen to the surface and the world is about to know what happened to that poor man. Whether it can be tied to me, I don't know. After so long, I doubt there'll be any evidence on the body. But I'm not a pathologist. I switch off the water and grab a tea towel to dry my hands.

The body in the reservoir.

Those words have echoed around my psyche for so long and now everyone in town, maybe even the country, will be saying them. But it's not their problem. It's mine. This is on me. Me and Dan. And any way that you look at it, it's bad.

It's very bad.

5

I t's the next day and I'm standing in the centre of my dad's bay window looking out at the sprawling hill-side when I hear the clink of crockery behind me. Turning, I see my old man shuffling into the room carrying a tray containing mugs of milky tea and a plate of biscuits. There's also a smaller plastic cup with a faded image of unicorns on the side that I presume contains milk or juice for Fern.

"Yey! Biccies!" she says as my dad places the tray down.

"That's right, darling," he says. "Help yourself."

"Just one, shorty," I add, but as Fern grabs for a pink wafer and a jammy dodger, I haven't the energy or impetus to stop her.

Dad catches my look and gives me a wink. "A little wafer isn't going to hurt, lad."

"*It's not going to hurt*, Daddy," she repeats and giggles.

I can't help but laugh with her. She's too cute. She's got me and Dad wrapped around her little finger and she knows it. Fern was supposed to be at pre-school today but two of the teachers have come down with a stomach bug, which has thrown the ratio of kids to adults off, so they asked if we could keep her at home. Jessie looked as if she was going to crumple when she got the call, but I was quick to tell her I'd bring Fern and Noah up to Dad's for a few hours. The little man is asleep – for once. He dropped off as we were driving up here and I carried him into the house in his car seat, which now sits in the corner of the sofa. I sit down beside him and check on him, before accepting the mug of tea Dad offers me.

"It's good to see you all," he says, taking the remaining mug over to his armchair along with a round biscuit wrapped in gold foil. "How's Jessie doing?"

"She's good, thanks," I tell him. Which is a lie. Even before Fern's pre-school rang this morning, I heard her crying in the bathroom. I tried to talk to her about it, but she brushed it off. At least for a few hours today, I can take the pressure off her a bit.

Looking after the kids also provides a welcome distraction, of course. I hardly slept last night after I got home. But I didn't need to fall asleep to be plagued with nightmarish images and thoughts of the past. Everywhere I looked in the darkness I saw his face and I could still hear the police sirens and the helicopter blades in my head. After a few hours, I got up and went downstairs, refreshed the local news app on my phone until Noah woke up around four and I helped Jessie feed him. There were no real updates in terms of the body in the reservoir. There still aren't. All the reports talk of human remains, but so far there's no link to any cold case. Whether it stays that way, who knows?

I sip my tea, watching my dad as he does the same. He always seems so strong and dependable. Infallible, even. I know that growing up, most kids feel that way about their parents, but I still feel that way about Jack Wilkes. He's a good man. Salt of the Earth. A better man than me. I sometimes joke he kept all the compassion and serenity genes for himself. But he was a great dad and he still is.

"Did you struggle?" I ask him. "You and mum. When I was a baby?"

I don't have any siblings. Growing up I used to wish I had a sister. But I think that was mainly because I liked the look of girls' toys and I wanted to play with them. These days it doesn't bother me either way and I suppose I like being my dad's primary concern – after Fern and Noah, of course. I've never asked him why he and mum never had more children, so I don't know if it was by choice.

"All parents have tricky moments," Dad says. "Your mother was wonderful with you, though. It was a different time back then. Men were more hands-off with the kiddies. But I did my bit. I fed you. I bathed you. I even changed your nappy a few times."

I grin at him. "A few times, hey?"

"Come on, now, they weren't these easy things like today with the sticky tabs and the like. We had terry towelling and safety pins to deal with."

I frown. "Really? I'm thirty-nine, Dad. Are you sure? They had Pampers back then."

"Maybe they did but we couldn't afford them."

He says it jovially enough but for some reason, the words land heavily and I have no response. Dad was a foreman at the local textiles mill for most of my childhood but was laid off when I was eight. I remember that was hard for a while. I used to hear him and my mum discussing things late at night when I was supposed to be asleep. But I never remembered raised voices or blame.

They were united in their troubles. A strong team, facing life's issues together. It makes me sad that it's not currently like that for Jessie and me. But like my dad always says, the best way around a problem is to take full responsibility for your role in its creation. If you accept that you're the problem, you can then be the solution.

When I get home, I'll sit down with Jessie, and we'll talk. Whatever's going on, together we can get through it.

I glance at Noah, who's got a strange smile on his face – which I suspect means he's recently filled his nappy. I'll change him in a minute. Fern is engrossed in deconstructing her jammy dodger biscuit and scraping out the creamy inside with her front teeth. I smile to myself. They're both brilliant kids and I am incredibly fortunate to have them. I need to remember that. Because with the drop in conversation comes an outbreak of unsettling feelings and troubling thoughts.

"Did you hear about the body they found?"

The words are out of my mouth before I know what I'm saying. I didn't intend to bring it up. In fact, I was hoping being here with Dad and the kids would be a welcome distraction. But perhaps a part of me wants to face it head-on. To call out the demon hovering over my shoulder and see what happens. Besides, if I don't talk about it with someone, I might go mad. If I'm not already there.

"In the dried-up reservoir? Aye." He sniffs. "I'd have expected them to find a few more bodies down there to be honest."

"Yeah?"

He sips at his tea. "Folk do silly things, don't they? Or folk do silly things to each other."

I stare at him, trying to work out his angle. He seems

quite blasé about the whole thing, which helps my mood somewhat. "What are you saying? You think there's been foul play?"

"Or they jumped in themselves."

"Is that what the police think?" I ask, somewhat eagerly.

"I've no idea. Maybe."

I so want this to be true. But I know the police would never think that once they'd examined the skeleton.

An image flashes into my mind. Of Dan and I dragging the poor bastard's body down the hillside. I remember I patted him down before we put him in the water. One of his legs was broken and his side was all crumpled in and sort of spongey and crackly when I touched it. I remember I was almost sick. I shake the thought away and place my mug down on the coffee table.

"Right," I say, slapping my legs and looking over at Noah, glad of another distraction. "I think this lad needs his bottom changing. But don't worry, I'll take him upstairs."

"If you're sure."

I stand and pick up the baby bag and Noah's carry seat. "Can I trust you two to behave yourselves while I'm gone?"

Fern looks up at me and then at Dad. He winks at her, and she giggles. "We'll be fine, won't we, Ferny?"

She nods. "Can I do some colouring in, Grandad?"

"Of course you can," he says, jumping to his feet. "Let me get your stuff."

6

As expected, Noah has done the mother of all poos. It's not quite the still-talked-about *Poomageddon,* which we had with Fern after she ate a whole punnet of strawberries, but it's not far off and has leaked out onto his sleepsuit. I lay him down on the bed in my old bedroom and inspect the damage.

How can someone so small, who's only ever ingested breast milk, generate so much of the stuff? He doesn't mind, of course. In fact, he looks rather pleased with himself as he lies there staring up at me, gurgling away. Maybe I'd be happy too if I'd just rid myself of so much noxious waste.

But I'm a dab hand at this sort of thing now. Holding my breath, I get him undressed and quickly bag up the offending nappy. Leaving the bag open, I go to work on his nether regions armed with a stack of baby wipes, placing each one in the bag once soiled. As I work, he continues to stare at me, blowing bubbles and smiling as he does.

"You're a happy little boy, aren't you?" I tell him. "You stay that way. Cutie pie."

I tickle his tummy and he giggles, and for a moment nothing else matters. Once clean I put him in a fresh nappy and one of the spare sleepsuits that we carry in the baby bag in case of such occurrences.

I pick him up and kiss him on his warm forehead before sitting down on the edge of the bed and cradling him in my arms. He's already drifting off to sleep and I should get back home soon. Next time he wakes up he'll want to be fed, and there'll be no consoling him when that happens.

A few minutes of quiet time up here won't hurt, though. As I rock my baby son in my arms, I cast my gaze around the room. This was my bedroom for most of my life, from the day I came home from the hospital as a baby all the way through my teens until I moved down to London when I was twenty – when life up north and the memories connected with it became too much for me.

I smile to myself. Dad has redecorated since then, the band posters and black and white striped wallpaper gone in place of neutral colours and tasteful decor. But I still feel safe here. Like I always did. In the sanctuary of my old room, in my old house, the horrors of the outside world don't exist. The body in the reservoir and the knowledge of what I did aren't real until I step outside.

I look down at Noah. He's asleep.

"What am I going to do, son?" I ask him. "If they find out I'm connected to the poor man in the water, I might have to leave you... and I don't want that. I don't want to leave you or your mum or your sister. I don't want you to grow up scared or worried or feeling guilty about anything. It's my job to make sure you're always happy. I want to be a good daddy. I want to be a good husband."

For a second I worry I'm about to burst into tears, but the feeling passes.

"It was an accident," I whisper to Noah. "We were stupid and we weren't watching where we were going. You see, my friend and I had been drinking too much. We thought it was a clear run home. It usually was. One road. There were never any police about, so we never thought twice about driving after a few pints. But we'd had a lot that night. But still, I thought my friend seemed fine to drive. And there was never anyone else around on that bit of road. No cars. And certainly no people. Not until that one night."

I close my eyes.

"I'm sorry," I whisper. "I'm so sorry." I'm not even sure whom I'm talking to now. Myself, maybe. Noah? The man in the reservoir? God? I've never been a religious man, but I've prayed these last few days.

Please don't let this happen.

Please let it all go away.

But it's not going away. None of it is.

I need to sort my head out. But first I need to sort things out with Jessie. If we can get to a place where we're on the same team again, I'll have a stronger footing to deal with whatever comes next. It's just that the way she stares at me sometimes freaks me out. It's as if she's trying to read my mind with her brainwaves. I get that she's still antsy and she thinks I'm keeping things from her. But I'm only doing it for her own good. I'm shouldering the problems so she doesn't have to worry. That's what a good husband does, isn't it?

My parents always seemed to face things as a united front – that was until my mum died when I was thirteen.

Cancer. Even then, though, I don't remember Dad missing a beat in terms of him caring for me. By that point, he'd got over losing his job and had retrained as a landscape gardener. He had his own business three years later. In the end, it was the best thing that could have happened for him. Being outside and doing manual work kept him fit and young, and I think provided a valuable focus for him to help deal with his grief. Or it was a useful distraction from his heartbreak.

Wilkes men. We're all about useful distractions.

"I'm going to make your mummy smile again," I tell Noah. "I love her very much and I need to make her realise that again. But you don't have to worry. Everything is going to be great for you."

There's no reason why Jessie shouldn't trust me. I've never and would never cheat on her. And I've told her everything. *Almost* everything. Besides, the person I was before I met her – reckless, toxic, a womaniser – that wasn't really who I was deep down anyway. I've come to suspect that this selfish and irresponsible version of Rob Wilkes was created by me to help deal with what happened. Before that night at the reservoir, I was a sensitive, deep-thinking soul. More like I am now, but with slightly less anxiety. I still worried about life and the future. I worried about my dad being on his own after Mum passed away. Then, when I was fifteen, I went through a phase of being a total hypochondriac. It was at the height of the Mad Cow Disease crisis, and I convinced myself I had it. I wouldn't consume or even touch anything that was remotely beef related. Which, living in a rural town in the peak district surrounded by moors and farmland, was rather tricky and painted me as quite an odd child to those who knew me. But I cared about things, is what I'm saying. Deeply. Then, after that night, everything changed. It was as if I saw the true evil of the world for the first time and it was so horrible I had to turn away. It was too scary to deal with. I didn't know what to do. I waited for the knock on the door – the police, coming to arrest me – but a week passed, then a month, and it never came. I'm not sure why.

That didn't mean I felt any better about what happened, however. If anything, it only exacerbated how I was feeling. I contemplated suicide at one point. I just wanted the nightmares to end. I tried to talk to my dad about it but I could only skirt around the subject. I couldn't tell him why I was feeling this way. But then, over time, I began to live more in the moment, focusing only on what was going on right in front of me. It was as if a part of me knew the only way I was going to survive and stay sane was if I didn't allow any thoughts or memories to occur. If they did, I diverted my attention to something else. Computer games, films, women. Mainly women as I got old. But true feelings were out of the question, too. So that meant I became very selfish and treated people badly. I was an awful person. Or at least, *that* version of Rob Wilkes was an awful person. But then I met Jessie Singer and everything changed again.

Our first few years together were amazing. I've always got on well with women but with Jessie it was like I'd fallen in love with my best friend. My best friend with whom I was able to have amazing sex. We became inseparable and, despite what I'd previously thought about needing my space, I didn't mind it one bit. I remember coming back to visit Dad one weekend early on in the relationship and pining for her the whole time I was here. She was funny, brave, intelligent, and she saw something in me that even I didn't see at the time. She challenged my thinking in so many different ways and I felt myself growing as a person in her presence. It's no exaggeration to say she saved me, and I'll always love her for that, no matter what happens. There's no way I'd have had the confidence or drive to open my own restaurant if it wasn't for her influence. She was amazing. She *is* amazing.

"I think she's worried I'm reverting back to my old ways, but I'm not that person anymore," I tell my sleeping son. "I just need to remind her of that. And I will. I'm going to sort this out. I promise."

I get up from the bed and go downstairs. It's almost two and I need to get back. I told Pearl I'd meet her at the restaurant at four to run through the menu for the Spanish night. At least that will take my mind off all this shit for a while. Another distraction.

When I get downstairs, I find my dad lying on the floor next to Fern, the two of them surrounded by felt-tip pens. Fern is colouring in a picture of some mermaids while Dad looks on.

"Look, Daddy," Fern says. "I'm doing this picture for you. Do you like it?"

"Aw yeah, darling. I love it. Thank you." My dad raises his head and grins. "We should get off," I tell him. "I've got to get to the restaurant in a few hours and Noah's going to need a feed."

"Right you are," he says, getting to his feet. He's still sprightly but I notice a grimace on his face, and he has to grab onto the coffee table to help him. He walks over to me and looks me dead in the eyes. "Whatever's going on, lad, you'll get through it."

I smile. It was stupid of me to think he wouldn't pick up on something. "Maybe."

"No maybes about it. You're a good man, Robert. I'm very proud of you." He grabs my shoulder and it's all I can do not to burst into tears.

"Thanks, Dad," I say, turning away from him. Then, to Fern, "Come on, trouble. Let's get you home."

7

I t's that night in Fire and Ice, as we're waiting for the first guests to arrive, that Carol informs me there was someone in the restaurant asking about me. An old friend of mine from way back.

"I remember," she says proudly, with a grin. "He was called Dan."

The name hits me like a brick to the face. "Dan? Are you sure?"

"Yep. Totally."

There are lots of Dans in the world. I wrack my brain trying to remember if I know any other Dans apart from *him*. There was a Daniel Simpson with whom I worked briefly at Clarington's in Mayfair. He was an odd kid. Quiet. I remember he always brought in his own knives from home and took them back with him each night on the tube. We didn't really get on. I can't imagine it would be him.

So that leaves only one Dan from my past. But of course it's him. For some reason, the universe has decided to fold in on me this week. I never believed in karma or anything like that, but it's hard not to at the moment. They say you reap what you sow in this life. Does that count if what you did was an accident? A mistake? Does it count if you've regretted it every single day of your life since? Even when I was living my life in such a whirlwind that I didn't have a chance to think about what happened, I still felt something inside of me. An insidious flutter in the depths of my belly. A knowing that I was unlike other people. I was tainted. Sullied by sin.

It must have been the same for Dan. If I'm honest, a part of me always expected he might come back into my life one day. We are forever linked. Forever bonded by what we did.

So, the sensation spreading through my body as Carol tells me Dan was asking about me and that he'd catch up with me later isn't one of shock or surprise. It's worse than that. It's dread. A deep, crushing dread.

He shouldn't be here. He shouldn't have come back.

"Did he say anything else?" I ask.

She twists her mouth to one side. "Don't think so." She lowers her chin and her voice, too. "Is he really a mate of yours?"

I scratch my chin. "He was. A long time ago. We grew up together. Why do you say that?"

She makes a face. "Nothing. It's just... he didn't look like your type of person."

"What's my type of person?"

"I don't know. But he was all scruffy and looked like he hadn't washed his hair in weeks. Plus, he had a weird way of staring at me. Deep blue eyes but sort of cruel and a bit creepy." She pulls her top lip back over her teeth. "Sorry,

Chef. I shouldn't say that about your mate. I'm sure he's lovely. I was probably in a bit of a rush and we got our wires crossed."

"Right. Yes."

She hurries away to get ready and after giving it a few seconds I follow her back into the kitchen. As I enter the corridor between the dining room and the kitchen, Simone walks out dressed for service.

"Shouldn't you get a wriggle on?" she says, nodding over my shoulder as I hear the front door opening and the excited hum of chattering guests. "The first covers are arriving."

"Yes. Will do. Thanks."

I leave her to welcome the guests and go into the kitchen. It's a thrum of activity and energy but I fail to match any of the exhilaration or enthusiasm. I head over to the blast chiller in the back corner and lean back against the wall.

Daniel Chapman is back in town.

And just like that, the world tilts on its axis.

Although, it wasn't always like this. Dan was my best friend in the entire world from the first day we met at the craft table in Mrs Aspel's class when we were five. From that day forward we were inseparable. Brothers in arms. Brothers from different mothers. We did everything together. Sleepovers, cinema trips, movie nights. At one point we started a band, but it never amounted to anything. It was fun. All of it. There was even a period of a few months when we were sixteen when I dated Sally Brandon and he dated Louise, her twin sister. We were so close. Right up until that night. Then we hardly saw each other ever again.

I think I've blocked out how truly awful that time was for both of us. I know we were both horrified about what we'd done but I don't remember whether we ever made a conscious decision to lie low and stay away from each other. But that's what happened. Not only did I lose a big part of myself that night, but I lost my best friend as well.

And, more importantly than all that, a man lost his life.

Not for a second did I ever think that I came off the worst. We killed someone and rather than ring the police and report the accident like we should have done, we filled his coat and trouser pockets with rocks and threw his body in the water. There's no excuse for what we did. But we were young and scared, and I for one wasn't thinking straight. Once it was done, we couldn't go back, no matter how much I wanted to. We had to try to live our lives as best we could. I recall that for a while I feared I might die too – if not actually by my own hands, then spiritually or mentally. I think I came close but eventually, the torment became too much, and I ran away to London in one last-ditch attempt to escape my life and what I'd done. I think I heard from someone that Dan joined the army around the same time. Probably for similar reasons. That was the last I heard of him. Until now.

A robust aroma of roasted garlic wraps itself around me. Normally I love the smell but today it makes me salivate in the way you do right before you throw up. I swallow it back as I rush through the kitchen and barge through the fire escape to the outside. The night air revives me immediately and I grip hold of the metal handrail that surrounds the top of the small decking area that looks out over the car park. I draw in deep breaths and exhale slowly, trying to calm my system. It's dark outside but still warm, and as my awareness spreads, I see a middle-aged couple getting out of a silver Mercedes. They look familiar. Probably they've visited the restaurant before, but I don't think I've ever spoken to them. The man nods at me as they walk down the side of the building towards the front entrance, and I smile and raise my hand in greeting.

My hope is I look like a hard-working head chef who's getting some much-needed fresh air – rather than a deranged freak struggling to cope with the egregiousness of his past mistakes.

I shake my head. What do I do?

Should I go looking for Dan and have it out with him? There's no way that him being back in town is a coincidence. He must have seen the news story and got the first train up here. Or down here, depending on where he's been living.

I can't figure out what his reasonings might be. Surely he's not planning to own up to the crime after all these years?

If he was, would I try to stop him?

Because what would happen if the truth was finally revealed? I expect I'd go to prison for some time, but what would Jessie think? What would my dad say?

A part of me believes that, if I explained myself to them in my own words, in time they'd understand and forgive me. Yet I've kept everything inside for so long that I don't know how I'd even start to tell someone else about what happened. And I doubt the police would be as understanding. It was an accident, but we were both drunk. That's bad enough. But dumping the body where it would never be found was no accident. I've wondered often other the years who the man was. Whether he had family, kids, or loved ones wondering and worrying about where he was. The conclusion I always come to – perhaps for my own peace of mind – is that he can't have had anyone in his life. Otherwise, there'd have been people looking for him. Glossop and the surrounding area is a tight-knit community. Even more so back then. We'd have heard something if a missing person had been reported. It's only a small consolation. Not really a consolation at all.

Wait...!

I straighten up as I notice movement across the far side of the car park. Someone is standing under the large tree in the far corner. As I snap my gaze over there they step back into the shadows.

"Hey!" I shout. "Who's there?"

There's no answer. And now, as I look harder, I can't even make out the shadowy figure I thought I saw moments earlier. I squint into the darkness. Did I imagine it? Is this my paranoid imagination playing tricks?

"Hello?" I call out.

Still nothing. No reply. No movement.

I walk down the three steps that lead onto the car park and stride quickly across the tarmac. Once I reach the tree I stop and peer into the space where the figure was standing. There is no one there. I throw my attention around the space as my breath comes to me in short, sharp bursts.

"Is someone there?" I ask. "Dan? Is that you?"

I walk right up to the tree and place my hand on it to steady myself. Beyond the car park is a patch of grassland and over to the left a small, concreted area that contains a rusty old swing set and a roundabout. One of the swings is swaying back and forth. But only one, and there's no breeze. It gives me the creeps.

"Dan?" I whisper into the blackness one more time. Then I turn around and, with my heart beating fast against my ribs, walk back into the restaurant.

8

W e're going too fast, taking the curves and bends in the road at too great a speed. I tell him to slow down. *Take it easy, man.* But he just laughs. He tells me I'm being a pussy. *Everything is under control.* But it's not. I know it's not. The feeling in my gut tells me it's not. We turn the next bend and then I see him. The man. Like always, he's dressed in a dark green jacket with the collar up. I don't notice what else he's wearing. I never do. As the headlights pick him out, he spins around but it's too late. It's always too late. Except in this version of events, time stops and the figure morphs into the dark form I saw at the far side of the car park. The figure has no features or details to his body apart from a withered hand, which he raises up from out of the void and points at me.

"You," his voice booms.

"No," I tell him. "No. Please. It wasn't me. It wasn't my fault. I'm sorry. I'm—"

Shit.

I sit upright in bed, eyes scanning the room for danger

as I fight my way free of the night terror. I see the chest of drawers facing the bed, the photos of Fern as a baby and Jessie and me on our wedding day standing on top. I see Noah's crib up against the wall and him inside making gentle whimpering noises. The warm glow of his night light arcs up the wall.

I'm safe.

I'm in bed.

In my house.

"Rob?!" I look over to see Jessie propped up in bed, resting her head on her elbow. "Are you awake? Properly awake?"

I nod. "Sorry. Another nightmare."

"Yes. I know. I heard you."

My heart still feels as though it's making a concerted effort to break out from my chest. "Ah, no. Was I saying things again?"

"Mm-huh," she says. "More than usual. Are you feeling okay?"

I frown. "Yeah. I think so. I just had one of my bad dreams."

"What happened this time?"

"Same as always. I felt like I was falling through the Earth. But it was just a feeling rather than images. Surreal. Like always." I've never been able to tell her the actual content of these nightmares for obvious reasons. Sometimes they are weird and ethereal. Sometimes they're far too realistic and exact.

"You kept saying sorry."

I look deep into her eyes. "Did I?"

"Who were you saying sorry to?"

I look away and shrug. "Shit. I don't know."

"Was it me? Were you saying sorry to me?"

"What? No. Why would I be?"

She flicks up her eyebrows in a way that tells me she's already played judge, jury and executioner in whatever trial she's imagined. "I don't know, Rob. You tell me."

I chew on my lip, telling myself it's just her old patterns coming back to haunt us. Those exes of hers have got a lot to answer for.

I lean into her. "Jessie, I've done nothing I need to say sorry for. I swear to you. Except for maybe not pulling my weight around here a little more. But I will do. I promise. Just as soon as I get the restaurant back firing on all cylinders."

She turns to meet my gaze. Her big, dark brown eyes – the same eyes that I fell so madly in love with – search my face, perhaps looking for a sign I'm lying to her. I smile back and think happy thoughts, hoping they show on my face.

"Jess. Come on. I love you. I would never do anything to hurt you or to jeopardise what we have here. Our little family is everything to me. It's all I've ever wanted."

"Who were you saying sorry to?"

"I don't know! I don't bloody remember!" My voice rises into a shriek. I take a moment and change tack. "Jessie – darling – it was only a silly dream. It doesn't mean anything."

But even as I say this, I know it's a lie. It means something. These dreams always do.

Jessie sighs and looks as though she's about to speak, but before she does Noah begins to cry. She rolls her eyes instead.

"Great. Now he's awake."

"Do you want me to get up with him?" I ask.

"And do what? He wants boob. That's all he wants."

She flings back the covers and cool air whips around my naked body. I've always slept naked. It makes me feel freer and less constricted. I also like the idea that at some point in my day, I will return to a more innocent and pure form. The way I came into this world, unfettered by immorality and the pressures of modern times. No doubt a therapist would have a lot to say about the reasons behind these ideas, but I've never seen one. Even when I was at my lowest point and actually thought seeing someone would help, I couldn't bring myself to. I was scared of what I'd say, and no website ever gave me a complete answer on what a therapist might do if I disclosed the worst of myself to them.

Jessie leans over the crib and lifts Noah out, placing his head on her shoulder and tapping him gently on the back. She makes shushing noises as she turns around to me and nods at the alarm clock next to the bed.

"I might as well get up."

I look at the red digits on the clock. 5:27 a.m. "Okay," I whisper as she leaves the room and goes downstairs.

I lie back in bed and close my eyes, but I know I'm not going to get back to sleep. Nor do I want to. Not if those same sickening images are on the other side of slumber, waiting to pounce.

I can still feel the remnants of the dream in my body. It was a particularly vivid one, and those tend to stick around. Become part of my psyche for the rest of the day. I sit up and lower my legs onto the carpet. The first rays of the day's sun filter through the curtains. It's going to be another hot one.

9

I've not been for a run in a while but the next morning I set my alarm for 5:30 a.m. and jump out of bed before I'm awake enough to talk myself out of it. I always find exercise does wonders for my mental health and ability to think clearly, and I hope that this is still the case.

Jessie is feeding Noah in front of breakfast television as I pass by the front room and gives me a funny look on seeing me dressed in running gear. I tell her I'll only be twenty minutes and then I'll look after Noah while she goes back to bed. When she doesn't respond, I take that as a green light and head out.

It's already warm and I head along my usual route, jogging down the side of the river and then back up the hill towards the high street. The incline is steep as hell. Steeper than I remember. I used to see it as a worthy challenge but today it almost kills me. I have to stop running a third of the way up and walk the rest of the way.

I'm more out of shape than I realised. When this is all over, when I've got more mental and physical energy available to me, I'm going to create a new exercise regime. I'm going to get fit. I need to.

But even as I think this, even as I'm striding up the hill clutching my side, I can't help but let out a bitter laugh.

When this is all over...

Who says it's ever going to be over?

At the top of the hill, I quicken my pace and even fall back into a jog as I get closer to home. Once there, I go straight into the lounge but Jessie isn't there. All being well, Noah fell asleep whilst feeding and she's been able to put him down and go back to bed herself. But then I hear voices coming from the kitchen and Fern's high-pitched giggle.

I put my head around the door to see the three of them sitting around the kitchen table. Noah is asleep in Jessie's arms and Fern is kneeling on her chair, bits of card and pots of glue and glitter strewn across the table in front of her.

Jessie looks at me with the expression of a world-weary stand-up comedian. "We're making a birthday card for Grandad."

"Look, Daddy," Fern says, holding up a card with a blue feather and some badly cut-out triangles stuck on the front. "It's a pony."

"I can see," I say going over to her. "It's amazing, shorty. Well done."

"I'm making one for you too next."

"That's great. Thank you. I'm so lucky." I raise my head at Jessie and give her a thin-lipped smile. Making cards. Fun times at six in the morning.

"Good run?" she asks. "I thought you were only going to be twenty minutes."

"Yeah. Sorry about that. I'm not as fast as I thought I

was." I grimace dramatically. "Do you mind if I jump in the shower? Then I'll make us all breakfast."

She snorts and looks away out the window, which I take to mean she does mind but she accepts it needs to happen.

I head upstairs and go straight through into the bathroom to switch on the shower. While the water warms up, I strip out of my sweaty clothes and stuff them in the laundry basket. As I step into the cubicle the water is still cold but it works for me. I put my head under and enjoy the cool jets as they revive my brain and stay this way until the water has heated up. Once it has done, I quickly wash myself and turn off the shower. It's time to start the day. Something tells me it's going to be a heavy one.

"Are you working today?" Jessie asks as I enter the kitchen. Her voice is steady and she smiles at me. Back to being nice Jessie again.

I walk over to the larder cupboard and open the door as I consider my answer. I wasn't planning on going to the restaurant until evening service, but if I say that she might have a list of errands for me and there are things I have to do today.

"I was going to ask Pearl to run the pass this lunchtime as practice for her," I say, not turning around. "But I'll probably still need to be there to supervise." It's a half-truth. Or a half-lie. Depends on your point of view. I glance back over my shoulder. "But I don't have to. I can be here with you if you need me to."

She shrugs in a resigned sort of way. "Whatever. Doesn't matter. He's still going to only want me, isn't he? Can you take Fern to pre-school and pick her up, though?"

"Yes. Of course I will. Can I take your car, so I don't have to swap her car seat into the van?"

She shrugs. "Don't see why not."

"Okay. Thanks."

I make us all eggy bread, which is Jessie's favourite, so I'm a little dismayed when she leaves half of it. I don't say anything. Instead, I stack the dishwasher, clear up Fern's craft stuff into her box and get her dressed and ready for pre-school. While she's cleaning her teeth – or, at least, whilst she's chewing on the toothbrush, which is the best I can hope for today – I examine myself in the bathroom mirror. It's never a flattering image in this light but I look particularly old and haggard today. It feels as if all the toxic thoughts and feelings currently filling my system are making themselves known on my face. I used to be a good-looking guy. I guess I still am after a good night's sleep and without all the stress weighing me down. But who cares about any of that? I've got much, much bigger problems than eye bags and thread veins right now.

After dropping Fern off at pre-school I intend to drive over to Dan's old house and see if I can find him. I know his dad died a few years ago and his mum sold the house and moved down south to be near her sister, but for some reason, I expect to see him there. He used to be always outside, playing in the back garden or sitting on the front step, looking out over the road. When we were young, he'd always see me as I appeared over the brow of the hill and would do this ridiculous over-the-top routine of waving and doing a silly dance. It was him trying to embarrass me, I think, but it never had that effect. I liked it. I used to pretend I was his long-lost sibling, returning from the war.

It feels a bit like that as I approach his old house. It's

the last terrace on the row before the road winds down the hill past the fire station, and I slow the car as I get up to the front door but don't stop. Instead, I carry on down the hill and up the other side, speeding up as I get onto Charleston Road. I drive through the next village and out the other side before taking a left onto a winding country lane only wide enough for one car, that curves around the edge of the Peak District National Park. It's a nice road with trees and fields on both sides. Newly born lambs frolic in green pastures whilst starlings and sparrows flutter and soar overhead. I've been on this road a few times before but not for many years. I'm not sure where I'm heading or even if I care, but after twenty minutes I pass the Wind In The Willows hotel on my left and decide to drive on to the reservoir.

Was that my plan all along?

Did my subconscious mind want me to drive here?

Back to the scene of the crime.

I turn on the CD player in an attempt to drown out these thoughts. The last thing I had on was *Rain Dogs* by Tom Waits and the next song up is *Hang Down Your Head*. The lyrics seem excruciatingly appropriate as I speed along with the volume up as high as it will go.

I get to Glossop town centre and take a left along the high street and then a right onto Woodhead Road, which takes me out of town and past the first two reservoirs. As I get up to the edge of Woodhead Reservoir and take the road that leads onto the A628, I can already see the police tape and a triad of crime scene tents at the side of the dried-up reservoir on the other side of the valley. I slow the car to a stop in a lay-by across the road from the over-flow outlet and get out. There's a breeze in the air here but it's welcome as I lean on the wall overlooking the scene. I can't see any movement going on near where the body was found, or even any police officers, but they might be inside the tents. I imagine the remains have now been moved elsewhere, however. Probably they're in a pathologist's lab over in Sheffield or Manchester, being poked at by some stern-faced doctor to try to establish the cause of death.

I shiver, which I want to believe is due to the cold wind whipping through the valley, but which I suspect is most likely an adrenaline response to being here. I stare out over the dry reservoir, trying to come to terms with how I actually feel about the situation. The truth is I have so many conflicting thoughts and ideas about it I'm uncertain. A small part of me is almost glad the body has finally been found. I hated thinking of the poor man being down there, with no one knowing where he was. At least now he can be laid to rest. Whatever that means. Yes, it's concerning – which is, perhaps, the understatement of the year – but I've done a lot of research since that night. I don't see how the police would be able to tie the body to me after all this time. Even if the body did contain paint remnants from my car, or DNA from when we carried him down to the waterside, time, plus twenty years underwater, would have eroded everything away. All they have to go on is an old skeleton with a few broken bones. Anything could have happened to that man.

I stay here for a while longer, I'm not sure how long, but by the time I climb back behind the wheel of my van the skin on my face is throbbing from the wind and sunshine. The clock on the dashboard tells me it's almost eleven, and lifting my phone from the passenger seat where I chucked it earlier, I see I've missed two calls from Jessie. A fresh wave of panic blossoms in my chest but I push it down before it has a chance to grow legs. It's probably nothing. Rather than call her back I decide to head home. It's only a ten-minute drive from here and whatever it is she wants to speak to me about can wait that long. As I start the engine, I realise I'm smiling. Considering everything that's going on, that surprises me, but you've got to stay positive, haven't you? Focus on what you can control. Right now, that means driving home to my wife and looking after her. It'll be a pleasant surprise for her. Maybe I'll even suggest we go out for lunch. Once she's fed Noah, he can sleep in his carry seat whilst we eat. It'll be nice. Like old times.

Motivated by this decision, I drive home and am still buoyant even as Jessie opens the front door of the house and hits me with a stern look.

"Hey," I say, getting out and slamming the car door. "I was thinking we could get a bite to eat. We could check out that new deli you were talking about. What do you think?"

She doesn't answer until I get up to her. When I do, she pouts her lips in a way that unsettles me. "We can't," she says. "We've got a visitor."

My stomach turns. My heart stutters. "Oh?"

"Yeah," she says, flashing her eyes at me like I've seen so many times when she's raging. She gives me a big, pointed smile, dripping with sarcasm. "Your friend Dan called around to see you. Isn't that great!"

DAN IS SITTING at the table as I walk into the kitchen. The first thing I notice about him is his hair. It's as thick and jet black as it always was, but the style is vastly different since the last time I saw him. He always used to wear it short and combed forward, but now the top part is long and straggly and swept back from his face and the sides are shaved almost to the skin. It makes him look like he should be sitting down in traffic, protesting about the climate crisis. The army fatigues and dirty red hoodie don't help his case.

"All right, mate," he says. "Long time no see." He grins, revealing two rows of yellowing teeth.

"Yep. Been a while," I reply, as Jessie shuffles into the kitchen and pushes past me. Because what else can I say when she's here? What I really want to ask is *what the hell are you doing here*? What I really want to do is drag him out of my house and tell him to never bother me again. "You look well," I say.

He scoffs. "Do I? Well, thanks. I suppose." He juts out his chin at Jessie. "Your good lady wife here was telling me all about what you've been up to these last ten years. Two kids. Nice house. And your own restaurant, too. That's amazing. I'm proud of you, man."

"Thanks. Yeah, we're getting there." Jessie sits in the chair at the end of the table. "Have you been here long?" I ask him.

"Nah. About a quarter of an hour."

"Nearly an hour," Jessie mutters, under her breath. She sits back and rests her hands on the table. Noah is asleep upstairs, but she looks frazzled. Like she could do with Dan being here even less than I could. "I need to eat something."

"Right. Sure." I pick up the kettle and walk it to the sink. "I'll make some tea and sandwiches."

Dan sniffs. "Lovely. Thanks, mate."

I can sense Jessie glaring at me, but I don't look at her as I fill the kettle and place it back on its heat pad. "So..." I

start but am unsure how to continue. Most of the questions I'd normally ask a long-lost friend on seeing them
again sit in dangerous territory. Or I already know the
answers.

What are you doing back here?

What have you been doing with yourself?

Why DID we ever lose touch?

"...It's good to see you, mate," I say. But I don't sound
very convincing.

"Aye, you too, Rob. You too. Look at you, all grown up.
Head chef. Restaurant owner. You must be doing all right
for yourself, hey?"

I turn back to look at him. He regards me with another
wide grin, but I sense malice beneath the surface. It's
unnerving but that's what he wants. He knows he's rattled
me by coming to my home unannounced. One wrong
word from him to Jessie and my life is ruined.

I make a pot of tea and a plate of cheese and pickle
sandwiches, and for the next twenty minutes we eat and
drink and make small talk. I hardly recognise Dan today.
Even his laugh sounds different. It's colder. More cynical.
But maybe that's understandable. He tells us briefly about
his time in the army – two tours of Afghanistan – but
doesn't go into much detail and I'm thankful for that. He
has a glimmer in his eyes that unnerves me. It's something
that I can't quite put my finger on, but it was never there
before. It's as if he's seen too much of the world and no
longer knows how to relax. The whole time he's talking I
nod along, acting as interested as possible to counter
Jessie's growing impatience. It's awkward as hell and I
don't unclench my stomach muscles or my bum for the
whole twenty minutes. It's exhausting. I laugh, I joke, I tell
a few old stories and even do bad impressions of a few of

my and Dan's old teachers. But inside I'm back to spinning plates. I have to ensure there are no uncomfortable lulls in the conversation. I'm anxious that at the first opportunity he gets, Dan is going to say something – or allude to something – relating to that night. Then the plates, along with my entire life, will come crashing to the ground.

"How's your mum doing?" I ask. Dan lowers his head and gives me a withering look.

"She's okay. I haven't seen her for a while."

"That's a shame."

I have so many questions – real questions, important questions – bubbling up inside of me that I'm struggling to cope. I sit back in my seat, smiling at Jessie and Dan in turn.

"We fell out because she got vaxxed. I told her not to, but she wouldn't listen."

I widen my eyes at Jessie, but her expression remains neutral. I know she wouldn't say anything, not to Dan's face at least, but I also know she has a lot of strong opinions about people like Dan, who get most of their information from YouTube. I'm also certain she'll have plenty to say about him once he leaves.

Dan was always a bit kooky – 'a bit leftfield,' as Dad would say – but I always thought the army would have slapped that out of him. It seems to have had the opposite effect. Some of the things he comes out with as he goes into a monologue about vaccines and the 'Big Reset' make me think he's turned into a full-on conspiracy nut. He's anti-vax, anti-government, anti-everything – or so it seems. He grows more animated as he talks, which only makes him appear more erratic.

Bloody hell.

What happened to you, mate?

I looked up to Dan my whole childhood. He was always cool as hell and charming with it. I spent most of my formative years in his shadow, but I liked it there. There was a lot of fun to be had being Dan Chapman's best friend. To see him now, wild-eyed and irate, upsets and scares me in equal measure.

"Where are you staying while you're visiting?" I ask him and immediately regret it. Out of the corner of my eye, I see Jessie staring into her hands. I tense and add, "I'm afraid we're all full up here, and with the newborn it's a bit of a nightmare, but..."

I trail off, unsure how to end that sentence, and at that moment my darling son, the apple of my eye, chooses to wake up and start screaming.

Thank you, little man!

Jessie scrapes back her chair.

"Do you want me to go?" I ask her.

"No. It's fine."

The room falls silent as she heads out and up the stairs. I wait to hear the creak of the landing floorboards before turning on Dan.

"What the hell are you doing here?" I rasp.

"You know why I'm here. You've watched the news, surely?"

"Have you? The way you were talking just now, it sounds like you don't trust the mainstream media. I'm surprised you even own a TV or a phone."

"Well, I do. It's important to know your enemy and all that. I have news alerts set up for this area. Just in case." He taps his finger against his temple. "I always thought... You know... It would all come out eventually. I came up on the first train I could get. I came straight to find you."

"Where are you staying?"

"I've been in Brighton for the last five years. It's all right. Although I've got a bit of heat on me at the moment so it's good to get away."

I sit forward. "What do you mean? Heat?"

"It's fine. It doesn't matter." He waves his hand dismissively. "Just some guy I owe a bit of money to."

"Right. I see. But I actually meant where are you staying while you're in town?"

"Ah. I'm camping up on the hillside. You know our spot, overlooking the valley."

"Bloody hell, mate. Get a hotel."

"Nah. It's cool. It's summer, isn't it? Nice and warm. And I like to stay incognito."

I sit back and fold my arms. "What the hell, Dan? You've changed."

"So have you!" He glares at me and I hold his gaze. I'm prepared to hold it for as long as it takes. I need to show him he doesn't intimidate me. Finally, he sneers and looks away.

"What's going on, Dan?"

"I had to come back. I had to see you," he says. "I've thought about it a lot over the last few years. It's started to eat away at me. Do you still think about that night?"

"Yes, of course I do."

"What do you think about?"

I shake my head. "That's a stupid question."

"Is it?" he snorts. "I suppose it's the guilt that eventually eats away at you. It's insidious. It takes away all your goodness. And your sense of right and wrong. It's not easy, living with what we did. You must feel it too. And now this... The spectre of our misdeeds finally rises from the depths of despair. That's enough to send any person a little doolally, wouldn't you say? That and being shot at by bloodthirsty IS soldiers, twenty-four hours a day for two years."

I exhale down my nose. I don't know what to say to this, so I don't say anything.

"What are you doing here, Dan? At my house. What do you want?"

"I wanted to see you. I wanted to talk to you. It's about time, don't you think?"

"What have we got to talk about?"

He laughs but manages to make it sound menacing. "Plenty, I'd say."

10

I stare across the table at Dan, doing everything I can think of to stay calm. I breathe in slowly through my nose and hold it for a few seconds before exhaling.

"I don't think we should be talking about this," I say. "I don't even think it's a good idea for us to be meeting up."

"No, Rob. We need to get our story straight. Just in case they find out that—"

"No. We don't," I whisper. My survival instincts have me glancing over my shoulder, but I can still hear Jessie pacing in Noah's room. "It's not going to come out, Dan. None of it is. That skeleton they pulled out of the mud is twenty years old. Maybe they'll be able to find out the man's name if he had dental records – and they'll know something bad happened to him, but that's all they'll know. You're not the only one who can use the internet. I've done plenty of research over the years. I really don't think we're going to—"

"What if I want to come clean?"

"Sorry?" I unfold my arms and sit forward. "Are you serious?"

"Maybe." He squints at me. "Maybe not. Don't you want to wipe the slate clean? Doesn't it eat you up?"

"It hadn't done. Not for a long time. Not until the bloody reservoir started to dry up. Fucking global warming."

He gives me a toothy grin. "Aye, don't get me started." He leans back and wrinkles his nose. "Why did you move back up here?"

I puff my cheeks out. Now there's a question.

The truth is I never planned to return to the area. I was done with the place. After moving to London at eighteen I worked in a few bars before I landed a job as a pot washer in Garrett's. Simon Astor had taken over as head chef a year earlier and had just won their first Michelin star. Astor was a good person to work for. He was firm but fair and seemed to like me for some reason. He took a chance on me and promoted me to the role of kitchen porter and then trained me up to be a junior chef. I loved it. After years of floundering, thinking I'd ruined my life before it had even started, I had a second chance. I threw myself into the role with everything I had. I lived and breathed being a chef. I watched videos, read books, ate out in fancy places as much as I could. After working for two years at Garrett's I applied for a job as chef de partie at the two-starred Barrington Hotel, working under Andre Allard, and became their new saucier. That was where I met Jessie. She was one of the waiting staff, working there to help pay the bills whilst she finished her Master's degree in Business and Management. She told me her dad had owned pubs her entire life and her dream was to open her own restaurant one day. I liked that idea. I liked her more. For the first time ever, I began to think about the future. By the time we were married, I'd got to the stage where I hardly thought about what had happened that summer twenty years earlier. I know that sounds terrible. But I am very good at compartmentalising my existence. It still stung when I thought about it, and every so often I'd have a nightmare that would floor me for a few days. But with Jessie by my side, I felt like a new person. I was reborn.

It was Jessie who first suggested that we move to Glossop. We'd visited my dad a few times and she'd begun to fall in love with the area. She loved the sprawling hillsides, the fresh air, the peace and quiet. After the third miscarriage, she decided we should move here and that was that. She'd convinced herself the fresh air would help, and maybe she was right. Fern was born sixteen months after moving back here.

"It was Jessie's idea," I tell him.

"I see. So, you just do as you're told now. Is that it?"

I chew on the back of my bottom lip. I can tell he's trying to get a rise out of me. Ever since I arrived home I've sensed a really nasty energy coming from my old friend, and now I realise what it is. Bitterness.

"So you've come back here to fuck my life up. Is that it?"

He scoffs again and wipes his hand across his mouth. "Not at all, mate. I'm here to talk to you. To figure something out. Together."

"There's nothing to figure out," I snap, before realising my voice has risen. I rub at my face and when I speak again my tone is soft and slow. "I mean it, Dan. Please."

He tilts his head from side to side. "I don't know, Robby. I feel as if this is it. We had a good run but it's time the world knows what we did. We have to admit who we are. It'll feel better if we own up, I promise. We need to cleanse ourselves, mate."

The bastard.

Cleanse ourselves? What would he know?

He lowers his chin and regards me with a smug, almost beatific expression that creases his wizened face. He thinks he's the goddamn oracle of truth or something. I fight a strong urge to launch myself across the table at him.

"It's easier for you, though, mate. Isn't it?" I say. "You've less to lose. Less to leave behind."

He sticks out his bottom lip. "Do you think you're the only one who's struggled these last twenty years?"

"No. I know it must have been hard for you as well."

"Do you?" he barks. "Do you know that? *Mate.*"

I hold his gaze, resisting the impulse to check on Jessie – and that she hasn't heard him. I relax my shoulders, hoping if I try to stay calm, he'll do the same. Dan doesn't blink.

"Being in Afghanistan must have been hard. It was a horrible time to serve."

"You can say that again. The army was supposed to be my get-out. My version of running away to London. But I came back more fucked up than when I joined up. I killed people. Lots of people. And I was paid to do it. Two tours." He shakes his head. "I saw a therapist for a while after I got back. But he was shit. He said I have PTSD. Maybe I do. I don't get rattled by car horns or any of that shit but there are days when I can't shake the images behind my eyes."

I nod, about to tell him I know what that's like. But I stop myself. Something tells me he wouldn't consider it the same thing.

"I'm sorry," is all I can think of to say.

"Whatever." He waves my empty sentiment away. "I've not been able to hold down a job since I got back. I get benefits. Some. But it's not a lot. For a long time, I thought there was something wrong with me. But now I think I've just got bad luck. There's bad juju hanging over me. And it all started that night. We shouldn't have done what we did, Rob. Ploughing into someone on a dark country road is one thing but dumping the body in a reservoir – that's bad. It's evil."

"Keep your voice down," I hiss, tapping the air with my hand. "Jessie is upstairs."

He sticks his bottom lip in an exaggerated show of contrition. I want to rip it off. "I need to cleanse my soul, Rob."

"No. You can't. And what we did wasn't evil. We were young. We were stupid. We weren't thinking straight."

"Weren't we?"

"So... what? Were we supposed to ruin both our lives, and our chances at a happy future, for one moment of foolishness? Yes, someone died. It was awful. But don't think I haven't felt the pain of what we did every day since." I lean over the table. "I've got a family now, Dan. I've got kids and a wife. They need me here. I can't go to prison."

"We might not do. If we explain what happened..."

I glare at him. Either he's being naïve, or manipulative, or he's more messed up and crazy than I first thought.

"We'll go to prison!" I assure him.

"Either way, we have to come clean, Rob. It's better we do it first, before they come for us. What's that buzz phrase all the shitty politicians use – *get ahead of the narra-*

tive. That's what we need to do. The police are going to find out. I know it."

"Please," I say. "I can't do this. It's in the past. Even with all this shit with the remains being found. It's still in the past. We're both different people now."

"We left the scene of a crime, mate. We were both blind drunk and we killed someone. And rather than report it we dumped the fucking body. That's messed up. We need to make amends. I need to do it. I've got to get rid of this bad luck. Whatever it takes."

He stands up from the table.

"Where are you going?" I ask.

He shrugs.

"Not to the police?" I get up and hold my hands out to him. "Don't do it, Dan. I'm begging you." He shrugs again and I lower my hands and make a fist.

"I need to get off," he says. "We'll talk again, okay? Soon."

"Where are you going?" I say. "How will I get hold of you?"

He strides over to the fridge where we have a magnetic wipe-clean 'Things To Do' message board. He unclips the pen and makes a big show of writing his mobile phone number on the board. "This is my number. I've not usually got any credit. But I can answer."

"Fine. Good. I'll ring you and we'll meet up again to talk. But don't do anything rash until we do. Promise me?"

He gives me a reassuring nod and taps me on the shoulder as he walks to the door. It's a pointed gesture, I feel, almost as if he's letting me know he's the one in control of the situation. And of my life and happiness.

In the doorway, he turns back and looks me up and down. "It is good to see you, Robby. It's been too long." I move towards him, but he holds his hand up. "Don't worry, I'll see myself out."

"Dan," I call after him.

"I said don't worry,' he replies. "Whatever happens, it'll be for the best. Trust me."

Then I hear the front door open, and he's gone.

11

We'd been at a live folk night at a pub in Holmfirth, the next town along. A bloody folk night. It hardly sounds like the flashpoint introduction to a tale of murder, secrecy and deceit, does it? I can't even remember the name of the pub. It's not there anymore. I do remember we'd got chatting with a couple of girls and we were buying them drinks. The plan had been to have two pints each, enough to feel it but not so much we couldn't get home. But as the conversation flowed and the girls became more affable, those two pints turned into four and then six. At one point, I did tell Dan I thought it was a bad idea for either of us to drive home but he said he wouldn't have to, that it was game on and we'd be staying over with the girls. Only, at the end of the night, they left without even a kiss goodbye. It turned out they both lived at home with their parents so any notion that we might both have a welcome bed for the night was scuppered.

Even then, I wanted to get a taxi back home. At least, I think I did. That's what I've told myself since. But Dan was adamant he'd be okay to drive home. We'd come in my car but after a brief exchange in the car park, I said he could drive it.

That was my first mistake.

Back in my kitchen I place the empty mugs and our plates into the sink and twist on the hot tap. As the basin fills, I squirt in some washing-up liquid. Out of the window, I see a couple of magpies perched on the wall opposite.

One for sorrow. Two for joy.

Is that a good omen? Either way, I know I can't let Dan go to the police. He seemed believable enough in his desire to own up just now, but I can't work out whether that's his actual goal or whether he's trying to mess with me. We were so close once, but I don't know him anymore. He's clearly a troubled guy and for now, I should take his threats seriously. My hope is I can reason with him. If not... I don't know what I'll do. I'll have to stop him some-how. I won't let him ruin my life.

As I continue to peer out the window one of the magpies flies away, leaving one remaining.

One for sorrow.

I switch off the tap and reach for the scouring sponge.

Normally I enjoy washing up. I like to make a game of it and give the process my full attention in a zen-like way. I find it relaxing. *Normally.* Today, as my sponge glides over the dirty crockery, more dark images and unsettling memories flash in my mind. I remember we had the car stereo turned up as loud as it would go. The Strokes had released *Is This It* the year before and I think it was what we were listening to. I remember we were singing along at the top of our voices, whilst laughing at our bad luck that evening. If only we knew.

We were almost home. We'd driven through Holme Moss and were on the part of the road that levelled off before it joined the A6024. Dan was joking around, swerving the car around to try to freak me out. I told him to stop. He did it more. We got to the point where the road curves around to reveal the reservoir at the bottom of the valley. He was laughing and looking at me for a reaction, so I saw the figure before he did. I cried out. Tried to grab the wheel. At this point, Dan must have seen the man too because he jerked the car over to the right and slammed on the brakes. But it was too late.

There was a dull thud – a noise far too muted for what it signified – and I saw a flash of dark green as the man bounced off the nearside wing. Dan brought the car to a stop but we didn't get out straight away. We just stared at each other with wide, terrified eyes. Panting, as our drunken brains tried to make sense of what had just happened.

I don't remember who got out of the car first. In fact, memories of what happened next are always hazy. There are images and feelings connected to what we did, but nothing concrete. Like, I don't remember who made the decision not to call the police. I want to say it was Dan, but that's probably self-preservation. I do remember the two of us approaching the body. I didn't dare breathe but winced as Dan rolled the man over. His facial features were hard to make out with only the moonlight to go on – which is why I know the image of his screaming face I see in my dreams is my imagination trying to mess with me – but I could see he was male and about fifty years old. He looked peaceful. But then I patted him down and felt the crunch of his ribs...

Whoever made the decision to put him in the water

did it fast. The next thing I know I'm holding the guy's shoulders and Dan has got his legs. I remember thinking how light he was. There was nothing to him. Thinking about it now, he was probably a homeless person, which was why no missing report was ever made and why we got away with it for so long. You might call that lucky. I don't.

I don't remember how we transported the body down to the A628 and over the bridge that crossed the reservoir. I do know for certain it was Dan who said we should put rocks in the man's pockets. I would never have thought of that. We filled them up with as many as would fit and then we hoisted the body over the side of the bridge and let him go. I think we were both in shock, because neither of us spoke. We just watched the body disappear below the murky water.

And that's where we hoped it would stay. That's where it had stayed.

Dan dropped me off at my house in the car and walked back to his place. I don't think we spoke even then. He just walked away into the night. After a quick inspection of my car, I went into my house. There was an indentation in the wing, but I'd already got that part of the story straight. I was going to tell Dad we hit a sheep. It was a common occurrence around these parts and he wouldn't think twice about it. So that's what I did, the very next morning. He was fine about it. He said he'd done the same thing a few years earlier and not to worry. I felt bad lying to him but I reasoned this way I was actually saving him a lot of pain and sorrow. And that's the way I've thought about it ever since. Dad got his friend, Malcolm, to sort the bodywork out and he removed all evidence of any collision.

"Has he gone?"

Jessie's voice snaps me back to the present. I jump a little but don't turn from the sink.

"Yeah, he had to get off." I pull out the plug to let the soapy water out and turn on the cold tap so I can rinse the plates.

"Thank God for that!"

Now I turn around. She's got changed from earlier and is wearing a pair of black leggings and an old sweatshirt of mine. "Did you not like him?"

"I don't like you whispering. What were you talking about?"

She stares at me as if waiting for an answer. "Nothing. We were just talking about old times."

"Old times? I see."

"No. Not that. I didn't mean that. Dan is a friend from childhood. I didn't know him when I was... you know, being a shitty person."

She lifts her chin. "Whatever. Noah's asleep, by the way. After he was sick all down me."

"Ah, shit. I'm sorry," I say, but she's already walked off into the front room.

I finish doing the washing-up and join her there a few minutes later. She's watching the local news, which is the last thing I need right now. I don't say anything as I sit on the sofa beside her.

"Careful." She budges up away from me.

I don't respond. She's having a hard time with things at the moment and my being secretive and weird is not helping.

"I'm sorry," I whisper as we both stare at the TV screen.

"What for?"

"Everything."

She laughs, humourlessly. "Anything specific?"

"No. Not really. But I know I should help out more around the house and with Noah. I will do. It's just hard at the moment with the restaurant. I promise I will off-load some of my responsibilities onto Pearl as we discussed. It's just... No. It's fine. I will talk to her. She's doing really well. I'm very lucky to have her."

"Oh. I see," Jessie snaps.

I look at her and frown. "What are you talking about?"

"Pearl. Lovely Pearl who you can't stop talking about. I bet you love working so closely with her."

"Jessie! Come on. It's not like that. Besides, I think she's into girls."

She makes a low harrumph sound. "It wouldn't stop you trying. I reckon you'd have a go at anyone given half the chance."

I stare at her until she looks at me. "Are you serious?"

She looks away and shrugs. "I don't know. I don't feel as if I know you anymore. I miss you, Rob. I miss us." She looks up at the ceiling as if trying to stop the tears from forming in her eyes. It doesn't work. A single drop runs down her face, which she makes no move to wipe away.

"Bloody hell, Jess. I miss us too. I love you."

"I love you too," she says. "It's just really hard right now. I've got all this shit in my head and I don't know what to do with it." She sniffs back and dabs at her eyes. "I'm sorry. I'm really sorry."

"No. I am."

I stare at her, not sure whether I should pull her close or leave her to work through whatever is going on inside her. The fact I pause and don't trust my instincts is probably another sign that things are bad.

Bloody hell.

Why is this happening now, on top of everything else? Is it Dan's presence? Is his arrival in town already a blight on my family?

But that settles it for me. I need him gone. And soon. I'm about to say something else, to try to reassure Jessie that she's got nothing to worry about, when Woodhead Reservoir flashes up on the screen in front of us.

Shit. What now?

I sit up and search on the sofa on either side of me for the remote control.

"What's going on?"

"I saw this earlier," Jessie says, seemingly okay with me again. "They think the man they found the other day had drowned."

What?!

I look at her. "Really?" My tone isn't as nonchalant as I'd tried for it to be. "How do they know that? It was a skeleton, wasn't it? Old remains."

"It's something about the bones. Apparently, modern forensics can tell even if prehistoric skeletons drowned because of these special algae that get into the bone marrow. It's pretty interesting."

"Right. Yeah. Sounds it." On the screen, a middle-aged woman with frizzy hair is talking to the camera in a laboratory. Then the shot cuts back to the dried-up waterbed where a section of police tape flaps in the wind. "So, they think he could have fallen in or committed suicide?"

"No. They say he had broken bones that had to have happened out of the water. The theory is that he was beaten up or hit by a car and then dumped in the reservoir. They say whoever did it probably thought he was dead."

"Shit," I mutter. But inside I'm screaming. "And they're certain of this?"

"Apparently. Because of this certain type of algae. I can't remember what they called it – but if it's present in the bones, it's likely the person drowned. Because if they'd died before being submerged, they wouldn't have swallowed any water. Something along those lines, anyway." She shudders. "Turn it off though. I can't deal with it. It's grim."

With pleasure.

I jump up and switch the TV off manually. When I sit back down Jessie is still facing away from me. I want to pull her close. I want her to hold me and tell me everything will be all right. But I can't ask that of her. Because I've no idea whether what will be the case.

Maybe Dan has something after all. Maybe we do need to cleanse our souls. We thought we were covering up a terrible accident for the sake of our futures, but that man might have survived if we'd only called an ambulance. He was still alive when we filled his pockets with rocks and sent him to his watery grave.

He was alive.

Meaning, we killed him.

Meaning, I'm a murderer.

I'M BACK at work the next day trying to hold it together, but it's hard. All I can think about is that poor man in the water. I have so many questions that will never be answered. Did he know what was happening to him? Did he wake up as his weighted clothes dragged him to the bottom of the water? And the one thought going over and over in my head more than anything else: He could have survived.

If only we'd called an ambulance.

If only we hadn't acted so selfishly.

After I moved to London I got really into existential literature for a while. I think it helped. I'm not sure. Books like Camus' *The Outsider* introduced me to new ideas and ways of coming to terms with the benign indifference of the universe. I convinced myself the man was already dead and there was no point in me dying a spiritual death also. And that's how it was for many years. I told myself it would be wrong of me – and even disrespectful to the dead man in the water – if I didn't try to live a good life.

But now that's all gone out of the window.

Knowing I could have maybe saved him makes me feel sick and angry and like I want to pick up an eight-inch chef's knife from off the counter and shove it into my stomach.

I have to sort my head out.

People are counting on me.

As well as the guilt crippling me, I can't stop thinking about Dan and his vague threat of exposing our dark secret to the world. He wouldn't do it. He can't. Someone like Dan wouldn't last five minutes in prison. I'd last even less. I've got to meet with him, reason with him. If I had money, I'd offer him that. Give him the incentive to keep quiet, buy his silence.

Shit.

What was that he said about owing someone money? Is that what he wants? Is that the real reason he's here? Blackmail.

I can't consider this idea for long as, at that moment, a plate of food appears before me on the pass.

"Erm, what is this?" I call out, turning to Lawrence, who has delivered it.

He glances at the plate, then at me, and his normally furrowed brow grows more pronounced. "Chicken Ballantine with morels and truffled cauliflower puree. Chef!"

I peer at the plate, then grab down the order tab from the line. "Table twelve?" I ask. "They want two of these. Where's the other? And where the fuck are the onion petals?"

Lawrence sniffs. "Sorry, Chef. I didn't—"

"You didn't what, Lawrence? Give a shit about doing a good job? You didn't listen? Which one is it? And this Provençale sauce is weak. Do it again! From fucking scratch! Jesus...!"

"Hey, hey." Pearl hurries over to me and grabs my arm, guiding me over to the far side of the kitchen. "Is everything all right, Chef?"

"No. It's not bloody well all right. I'm trying to run a professional kitchen here and my staff seem hell-bent on screwing things up. How are we ever going to elevate this restaurant to the standards required if they can't follow simple bloody instructions?"

Pearl waits until I've finished my tirade, then shifts around so she's looking into my eyes. "What's going, Rob? This isn't like you."

"What? Don't I usually want perfection for my dishes?"

"Yes, but you don't carry on like this. You told me when I started that you never want to act like a chef cliché. One of those red-faced wankers who thinks that shouting at teenagers and making people cry makes them look manly and powerful. And you haven't done that. You don't do that. Which makes me think there's something else going on right now."

Her words catch me off guard and for a second, I'm scared I'll burst into tears. I look away and wipe the back of my wrist across my forehead. "Maybe," I say.

"Yeah? Do you want to talk about it?"

"No." I still can't look at her. I rub at my face and the blue plasters I'm wearing on the first two fingers of my left-hand scratch the thin skin of my eyelids. Cutting myself twice in one day, after all these years, is probably another sign my mind isn't on the job. I sigh and give Pearl a redundant smile. "I'm fine. Thanks. I just needed a time-out, I think."

"Why don't you have a sit down for ten minutes – in the office?" Pearl suggests. "It's fine. I'll handle the pass while you get your head together." She lowers her head, regarding me with those intense brown eyes of hers. "Go on, Chef. I can handle things."

I glance over my shoulder at the kitchen. Everyone is at their stations, doing what they should be doing. Lawrence appears at the pass with two new plates of food. He looks cowed as he shuffles away and I hate myself for being such a prick to him.

"Okay," I tell Pearl. "Thanks. I probably do need a few minutes. I'll speak to Lawrence and apologise once I've calmed down."

She smiles. "He'll be fine."

I look back at Lawrence, hoping he'll catch my gaze so I can give him a nod of reassurance or even a sorrowful smile. But he's got his back to me stirring a pan of sauce. Fine. I'll speak to him later. I offer the reassuring nod to Pearl instead and walk through the staff room and into the small room at the side of the restaurant that I use as an office.

The space is cramped, with a desk along one wall and two filing cabinets opposite, with just enough gangway in between for a chair. I flick on the light and sit. The desk is strewn with papers – delivery receipts from suppliers, mainly, along with bills and invoices and bits of scrap paper containing scrawled ideas for new dishes. I lean back in the chair and heave out a long sigh, shaking my head at the mess in here. Once I have some free time, I'm going to get it looking decent again. A tidy office equals a tidy mind. Isn't that what they say? It's a saying similar to Dad's favourite quote about busy hands, but neither maxim fills me with much confidence presently.

Keep your friends close and your enemies closer – that's another one. I think of Dan. So, which is he? A friend or an enemy? Maybe he's both.

I pick up a handful of receipts and shuffle them into a pile. Underneath I see there's a stack of unopened mail that I wasn't aware of.

"Fucking hell," I mumble to myself. "How am I supposed to run a business if people don't give me the bloody..."

I catch myself. It's not doing my stress levels any good, focusing only on the bad stuff. Positive thinking is important. It's the only way I'm going to get through these next few days.

How we do anything is how we do everything.

I suck in a deep breath and open up the first envelope. It's an electricity bill. An astro-bleeding-nomical electricity bill. For almost double what it was for this period last year. Prickly heat erupts across my chest and up my neck. I place the bill to one side. I'll deal with it later. The next two envelopes contain bank statements for our business account and the main credit card. I speed-read them, but the information doesn't infiltrate my over-crowded mind. I already know we're struggling; I don't need to see it in black and white. I place these with the electric bill – to be dealt with at another time. The last envelope is the shape of a birthday card rather than a bill. I lift it and turn it around. It's sealed but there's nothing written on the front, no name, no address. It must have been delivered by hand if it was delivered at all. I glance out of the door, wondering if it's meant for one of my staff. A thank you card, perhaps. But screw it. It was on my desk.

I tear it open and slide out the contents. Inside is a single piece of white paper, folded to fit in the envelope. I open it out. My first thought is – I really hope it's meant for one of my staff. But I know it isn't. It's for me.

On the piece of paper is a message, made out of letters that someone has cut out of a magazine. It's the sort of thing you see in old movies – a ransom note sent from a kidnapper. The coating on the letters shines in the light as I hold up the note.

I KNOW WHAT YOU ARE

The *K* is made out of the *Kellogg's* logo. I don't know why I notice that; maybe it's me deflecting again. I stare at the paper for a long time as I wait for my stressed-out brain to catch up.

What the hell is going on?
Who knows what I did?
Dan?
Someone else?

A noise from the staff room startles me and I quickly fold up the note and stuff it in my lap.

"Hello?" I call out.

"Just me, Chef!" It's Simone. She's in the staff room next door. "I'm looking for a charger. One of the iPads is nearly out."

We've recently invested in new Point-of-Sale ordering software, which is great and gives the restaurant a high-end feel. But, post-pandemic, it's not as crucial as we thought it would be and it's more expense I don't need.

I hold the note in my lap. My heart is beating so fast that I feel as if I'm about to take off and fly into the ceiling. I swallow. "Have you tried behind the bar?" I ask her.

"It's okay. Found one. As you were."

I hear the door slam against the side of the wall as she leaves the room, but I wait a few seconds and lean over to fully close my office door before opening out the note again.

I KNOW WHAT YOU ARE

It's so cliched and almost ridiculous to look at, but, regardless, I feel an icy chill run down my neck.

It's from Dan. It has to be. It's his idea of a joke. The sickest of jokes.

I take my phone out of my pocket and open up my contacts list, glad that I had the inclination to get his number before he left the other day. I hit the call button and press the phone to my ear. It rings twice but then goes to an answering machine. I chew my lip as the robotic voice regurgitates the default message and I wonder if I should leave a message or not. Then the beep goes, and I find I'm talking.

"Hey, it's me, Rob. I got your little note. Well done. Ha ha. Now stop it, Dan. I mean it. It's not cool. I don't know what the hell you think you're playing at but please believe me when I say you have to stop. For both our sakes. Or else...Well, I don't know. But I've got so much to deal with at the moment, mate, like you wouldn't believe. So, please. No more. If you want to meet up and chat, then let me know. I'll be there. But no more stupid notes." I sit back, about to say more when another beep signals that I've filled my message limit.

Bugger.

I hang up and stare at my phone screen. Should I call back and say more?

I chuck the phone onto the desk. No. I've made myself clear. Hopefully, Dan will get the message and grow up now. I push off the desk and get to my feet. That wasn't the restful time-out Pearl was hoping for me, but I need to get back to work. At least if I'm working, I've got some means of distracting myself from all this shit.

Busy hands, quiet mind.

Yeah, right. I wish. I switch out the light and am about to leave when my phone begins to vibrate on the desk. Grabbing it up, I see Dan's name on the caller ID. I tap on 'answer call' and he's already speaking as I bring the phone to my ear.

"Were you threatening me just then?"

"Sorry? What?"

"In this little message you left me just now. 'You have to stop. Or else.' What do you mean by that? And what's this note you're talking about?"

I rub my face. Is he playing dumb? Messing with me? I decide not to give him the satisfaction of rising to his bait.

"What are you calling me for, Dan? I thought you never had credit."

He lets out a nasty laugh. "I got some. And you rang me first."

"Yes. I did. And now you've called me." I have a strong urge to chuck my phone against the wall. I can't deal with this.

"We need to talk," Dan says, and his voice sounds as serious as I've ever heard it.

"Yes, fine. I agree. I can do tomorrow—"

"Now. Come and see me. We can talk properly up here, away from the world. You know where I am. Near to the rocks where we always used to sit."

"Dan, I've got service. I can't..."

"We need to talk. I'll be here."

"Mate, I'm sorry but—shit!" He hung up. I grit my teeth so hard a sharp pain shoots up into my gums. I consider calling him back but I've got a strong feeling he won't answer.

But we do need to talk. I go into the staff room and grab my jacket. Through the door, I can see Pearl standing in front of the pass. She seems to be handling things well, and as I'm watching she sees me and gives a thumbs up.

"I need to pop out for half an hour," I mouth at her, accompanied by an exaggerated mime, me pointing to the back door and then at my watch. She seems to understand and replies with a double thumbs up.

I know she can handle it. Good.

Now I have to hope that whatever Dan has to say, I can handle that, as well.

12

I know exactly where Dan has set up his camp. He's
high up on the hillside, above where Woodhead
Road curls around in a severe hairpin bend. The
spot is flat and rocky and looks out over Rhodeswood, the
second of the four reservoirs. It's where we used to always
hang out, first as adventurous ten-year-olds on their first
quests without supervision, and then as angst-ridden
teens, trying to make sense of themselves and the world.
Most Friday evenings after dinner, the two of us would
climb up there and sit on the same two rocks. Dan had his
rock. I had mine. Often, we'd share a bottle of cider that
one of us had managed to obtain from old Geoff at the
local off-licence, despite neither of us being old enough to
legally buy it.

Sure enough, as I climb over the lip of the hillside, I
see Dan sitting on his rock. It's gone seven but being
summer it's still light. Dan is smoking something which
could be a hand-rolled cigarette or a joint but being up-
breeze from the smell, I can't tell which. A dark blue dome

tent is pitched up on the flat terrain a few metres behind him. Dan sees me and holds up his hand.

"It's like we've never been away," he says as I get closer. He finishes the cigarette – I can smell it now – and stubs it under his boot. "Do you like what I've done to the place?"

He casts his arms wide as if welcoming me to the area.

"It looks the same as it always has done," I say, sitting on my rock.

"It does, doesn't it?" He wrinkles his nose. "It's nice, that. Makes you realise, whatever you do, wherever you go, some things don't change. I find that rather reassuring."

"Good for you," I say, not caring how sarcastic I sound. "How long do you think you'll be here for? It can't be that much fun."

He shrugs. "Each to their own, mate. I like it."

"What if someone sees you and reports you? It's not legal to camp out here."

"Oh, bloody hell, is it not *legal*?" he mocks. "Don't worry, lad. It's remote enough I should be fine for a while, away from the eyes of the world."

It's not the answer I was hoping for. I take a moment to compose myself before I ask, "Why did you come back?"

"This is my home."

"Is it? I thought you lived in Brighton."

"Yeah, for now. Who knows where I'll end up? I like to live the life of a nomad these days. I find if you stay still too long in one place the badness begins to take hold of you. It's better to keep moving. That way, you cheat the devil. He can't catch ya."

I narrow my eyes at him, unsure how serious he's being. He looks like he means it. But if so, that's even more worrying.

"I don't think it's good that you're staying here," I tell him.

"Yeah, well, it's not up to you." He chuckles to himself. "Do you want a beer?"

"No, thanks. I stopped drinking."

He leans back and regards me with a crooked smile. "Seriously?"

"I've not had a drink in twenty years, mate. I've not had one since that night."

He whistles. "Wow. Fair play, I suppose." He gets up and staggers around the rock. Picking up a carrier bag, he pulls out a can of Guinness. "Do you miss it?"

"No. Not really. Sometimes."

"Yeah. Sometimes. Times like this, eh? When the shit's about to hit the fan?"

"Is it?" I ask, riled but glad that we're getting into it. "Did you send me the note?"

"Again, with this note business. What are you talking about?"

I stand and pull the envelope out of the back pocket of my jeans. Sliding the paper out from inside, I hand it to him. "This note."

He takes it from me, and I don't take my eyes off him as he reads. A scowl cracks his forehead and then the corner of his mouth twitches. "You think I did this?"

"Did you?"

"No! Where did you get it?"

"Someone must have pushed it through the letterbox at the restaurant. There was no name on it, but I assume it's for me."

Dan continues to stare at the note, sticking out his bottom lip as he does so. "This is the first time I've seen this, mate. I swear to ya."

For some reason, I believe him. "Are you sure?"

"I think I'd remember cutting out the letters and sticking them down, Robby. I'm no good at art. You know that. Here." He hands me back the note and I take it and put it back in its envelope and into my pocket.

"If you didn't send it... then who did?"

He looks at me as I sit back down. "I've no idea, mate. But someone knows. I don't know how, but they do. And this is why I wanted to talk to you. We have to own up. We have to go to the police before it's too late."

"No, Dan. We can't. I can't. I've got—"

"Listen to me, mate. If we go in and see them and tell them what happened, they might be more lenient on us than if they find out another way." He shakes his head. "We should have done this twenty years ago. I wanted to."

The words hit me hard. "What? No, you didn't."

"I did! Don't you remember? I came to see you the day after. I said we should turn ourselves in."

I open my mouth, but no words come to me. I can't actually believe what I'm hearing. Does he really believe what he's saying? I cast my mind back, trying to recall the events of that time. I remember waking up the day after the accident with a sense of dread hanging over me, but not sure exactly why. Then it hit me, like a brick to the face. Like a speeding car.

But I stayed in my room for the rest of the day. Alone. I told my dad I was unwell. I have no recollection of Dan coming over. I've certainly no memory of him saying we should go to the police. In my version of events, we didn't speak again. Back on the hillside, I tell him as much.

"I don't think we could face each other," I add. "We were too fucked up."

"No. That's not how it happened. You're remembering

it wrong. I came around to your house. Your dad let me in.
I wanted to confess but you talked me out of it. You said if
we held our nerve, we'd get through it. You were right, I
suppose. For a long time, at least."

I get to my feet. I can't hear this. He's wrong. He's
making up shit. Gaslighting me. "I don't understand what
you're doing back here, Dan," I say. "You don't really want
to go the police, do you?"

He looks away and pulls a face. "I don't know. I want to
do something."

"What the fuck does that mean?"

He leaps up off his rock and comes at me. "It means
my life is shit. It means everything that has happened
since that night has been bad. What we did fucked me up,
Robby. I can't cope anymore. This is a sign. A sign that we
need to speak our truth finally."

He leans forward. We're about the same height and
I'm probably a stone heavier, yet I feel uneasy as we face
each other. There's something in his weathered expression and watery but penetrating eyes that makes me think
he could snap at any second.

"Please, Dan," I say, lowering my voice. "We have to
leave it alone. Nothing ties us to that body they pulled out
of the water. Nothing. What we did was appalling and
stupid and I hate myself for it. But it's done. Us going to
prison isn't going to bring that person back to life. Ruining
our lives won't change anything."

"Ruining our lives?" Dan says. "I don't have a life to
ruin, mate." He stares deep into my eyes, and I think
he's going to hit me but then he sneers and sits back
down.

I wait until I'm sure I'm not shaking then sit also. We
both stare at the grass around our feet as a heavy silence

descends over us. It was a warm summer's evening as I trekked up the hillside but it's getting cooler up here.

My brain swirls with things I should say but nothing of use comes to me. "You do have a life," I mutter, finally.

Dan scoffs. "Do I? It's all right for you, Rob. You really do seem to have moved on. You've got a nice wife, lovely kids, and a good job being your own boss. You've done great for yourself."

"Actually..." I start, but he talks over me, so I shut up.

"You see, for me... I never could get my head straight afterwards. I had a few jobs, but I couldn't focus on anything. Careers, money – it all just seemed pointless. I thought joining the army would sort me out. I'd be doing something important with my life. Fighting for my country. But it only made everything twenty times worse. I killed people over there. Lots of them. No civilians, but men with families all the same. With kids and dreams. Who's to say they weren't chasing a stupid ideal same as me? I had friends die over there, as well. One guy, a Scottish lad called Drew, died in my arms."

I suck air through my teeth. "It must have been awful."

"It was. But do you know what? Those nights when I can't sleep, when I'm haunted by the past, it's not the faces of my fallen brothers that I see in the darkness, or even the Afghans I killed. No. It's the face of that old man, right after we tossed him in the water. I can see it now in my mind, his white face disappearing into the gloom. That wasn't an act of war, mate. We killed someone. Yes, it was an accident but that's no excuse. And now they're saying he might have been alive when we threw him in."

Bugger. He's heard the updates. I was afraid he would.

"They're not certain," I try. "Are they?"

"They seem pretty certain. And you know what that

makes us?"

I nod but I don't look at him. I can't.

"Does that make it worse?" I ask, even though I know the answer.

"Yeah, probably," Dan says. "I don't know anymore. I don't know anything. All I know is that as soon as I heard the news about that body being discovered, I was compelled by a force greater than me to come back. I need to face up to what I did. What *we* did."

"Dan, I've got a three-week-old baby." I turn to him. "I can't go to prison. I can't do this. I appreciate what you're saying but it's out of the question. It sounds as if you've had a really shitty time of it, and I'm sorry you had to go through so much pain."

And I mean what I say. The poor guy has obviously got PTSD. You can see it in his eyes. There's a glassiness to them that was never there before. It's as if a part of him is always watching something only he can see.

"Maybe I can help you," I tell him. "I *will* help you. We'll get you some proper support. But please, don't do this. We don't need to. We've suffered enough, don't you think? Dan? Dan, look at me."

He slowly raises his head to meet my gaze. "How can you help me?"

"In any way I can. Whatever you need. But don't go to the police. Promise me." I'm all but pleading with him on my knees at this point. I'm ready to tell him anything if he agrees to keep quiet. "Come on, mate. I'm on a fucking knife's edge. You think my life is going well, but it's not. Not really. One more thing and it could explode. I'm begging you. Go back to Brighton, forget about the body in the reservoir. We'll keep in touch from now on. I'll help you get better. I promise... Shit!"

The intensity of the moment shifts as the irritating electronic chime of my phone's ring tone pierces the air.

I stare at Dan. He nods at my jacket. "You should get that."

"Yeah. Sorry. One minute."

I pull it out of my pocket and see it's someone at the restaurant calling. "Hello?" I say, on picking up.

"Rob, it's Simone. Sorry, Pearl said you nipped out – but are you planning on coming back here tonight?"

I turn away from Dan and lower my voice. "Why? What's happened?'

"It's nothing major. The new girl, Danielle, who's been doing the lunch service, is in. Apparently, she didn't get paid this month and you told her she would be." I screw up my eyes, trying to focus on what Simone is telling me.

"Yes. She should have been. Does she need me to sort it tonight?"

I can almost hear Simone's face contorting in awkwardness. "It's just... She's come into the restaurant with her dad. They're still here, sitting by the bar. It's all fine and I've smoothed it over, but I think it'd be good if you came and spoke to them. Sorry, Chef. I know you're going through it a bit at the moment."

"Do you? Who said I am?"

"Oh. No one. I just mean...Well... You've looked tired and a bit distracted this week. No one blames you, of course; you work damn hard and with a newborn at home now as well..."

"Sorry, Simone," I tell her. "I didn't mean to snap at you. I suppose I am a bit stressed with one thing and another." I look back over my shoulder at Rob. Clearly, he's been listening to my conversation. He raises one eyebrow at me like he used to in class whenever David Cartwright would go off on one about politics.

"Give me half an hour," I tell Simone, getting to my feet. "Do you think you can placate them until then?"

"Sure. And I'm sorry for calling you."

"No. It's fine. I'm on the rota. I should be there anyway."

"Thanks, Rob. See you soon."

I hang up.

"Duty calls," Dan says, in a silly voice.

"Something like that." I grimace. "Are you going to be all right?"

He shrugs.

"Dan, will you promise me you won't go to the police? A few more days and this will all blow over, I'm certain of it."

He stretches his head back and blows out a long breath that makes him look a bit like a werewolf howling at the moon. He's not well. I see that now.

"I'll help you however I can, mate. I promise. Me and you, we'll sort it. Okay?"

He shrugs again. "Whatever, yeah."

I hold my hand out to him. "So... No police?"

He nods. "Don't fret, lad. If you really want to help me, then I suppose it doesn't have to come to that. I appreciate it."

I hold his gaze for a moment before I feel the pull of the restaurant. More stress to deal with.

"I've got to get off," I say. "I'll see you soon." I bang my fist on my chest. "Keep the faith, bro, yeah? We've got this."

Then I pocket my phone and head back down the hillside to the van.

13

A s I jump in the van and drive back to the restaurant Dan's words echo around in my head.

If you really want to help me...it doesn't have to come to that.

It's a big relief. He's not going to go to the police. Not yet, at least. But the panic and despair that had been plaguing me now give way to feelings of confusion and anger.

Was this his plan all along?

Is this the reason why he's come back after all these years?

These questions swirl around in my head until I get back to town and am driving down the high street. The police have set up what looks like a temporary drop-in unit in Norfolk Square and the sight of it makes me slow down. The unit is a shipping container, painted pale blue and navy and with a laminated sign near the door that reads *All Information Welcome*. Inside the lights are on and I can see movement.

My heart thumps in my chest as I bring the van to a stop outside the market hall. It's gone eight and service will be in full swing at the restaurant, but I need to know. I turn off the engine and jump out, skipping across the road and up to the entrance of the unit. The door is open and as I approach a woman with a kind face appears from inside.

"Is everything okay, sir?" she asks.

"Yes. Fine."

I peer over her shoulder into the cabin where I count four desks complete with computers but with only one of them occupied. He's a man about my age, dressed in a dark blue jumper. He's on the phone but looks bored as hell to be there.

"Is this always here?" I ask the woman. She's wearing black trousers and a cream blouse. Not what I'd call a police uniform.

"It's a new initiative," she says. "We're appealing for information to the local community regarding the human remains that were uncovered recently. The body in the reservoir." Her tone gets more serious as she says this, but her expression remains sunny. I get the impression she's a volunteer rather than an officer.

"Ah, I see." I decide to push the matter. "Have you had much information coming in?"

I'm pushing my luck being here, asking these questions. But I can't help myself. I need to know.

The woman lets out a sigh, but her smile strengthens if anything. "It's an ongoing investigation," she says. "But any information on who that poor individual might be, or what happened to them, will be greatly received."

"Yes, of course. I'm sorry, I have no idea. I'm only new

to the area in the last five years. I understand the body is quite old?"

She drops my gaze. "We're still gathering evidence, sir."

"Of course. I'm sorry for asking. But you haven't identified them?"

My hope is I'm coming across as a bored busybody rather than someone connected with the crime. I smile and fidget and wring my hands together. I feel this helps my case.

"Not yet," the woman replies. "That's why we're here for the next week or so, to ascertain what we can do about him and why he was there."

"You're doing a good job," I say, backing away. The fact they're here at all appears to be both a blessing and a curse. A blessing because it tells me that they're low on leads and information. A curse, because the longer they're here the higher the chance someone might remember something.

Yet I'm still adamant there was no one else around that night. For the last twenty years, I've wracked my brain and tried to remember if I saw anything – lights from a car in the distance, other people on the road. Nothing comes to mind. As far as I recall there were only three people in the area. Then there were only two.

I say goodbye to the woman and hurry back to my car, before driving the short journey back to Fire and Ice and parking in the car park. I enter the restaurant through the back door and after a quick check on the kitchen and to thank Pearl for doing such a sterling job at running the pass, I head through into the main space. Danielle is sitting at the bar as I get there, looking bored. A large man, who I assume is her dad, paces up and down behind her. He stops pacing as I walk up to him and regards me with a scowl.

"You the boss?" he says.

"That's right, Robert Wilkes." I hold my hand out to him.

He has a face like a fist and as he reaches for my hand his forearm ripples with sinews. Bulbous veins snake up under the sleeve of his Ralph Lauren polo shirt. Over his shoulder, Danielle shifts uncomfortably on a bar stool. I appreciate now that their being here is all the dad's idea.

"I hear there's been a bit of a mix-up?" I say, trying to remain calm as he squeezes my hand and steps towards me in a combative manner.

"My girl hasn't been paid," he says, releasing his grip and tilting his head to one side. "You owe her two weeks' wages."

Despite everything going on inside of me, I keep my cool. I've long since learnt that there is no point in meeting these sorts of problems with the same energy that created them. He's angry, he wants conflict, and I won't give it to him.

"That's terrible." I lean around to catch Danielle's eye. "I'm so sorry, Dani. That isn't right. How much is it you're owed?"

She looks nervous. Or embarrassed. It's probably a bit of both.

"Erm. I think it's for seven shifts. Yeah. Seven."

"I see. Well, let's sort this out for you." I look from her to her dad. "As you're quite new, I imagine the forms haven't reached payroll yet. But that's not your problem." I walk around the back of the bar and open the till. I'm relieved to see there is a stack of twenties and tens in two of the compartments.

Going up into my head, I do the maths. Danielle is only eighteen and the minimum wage for her age group is a paltry six eighty-three an hour – but I start all my staff on the living wage of nine pounds fifty an hour, rather than what I can get away with. I know what it's like starting as a kid in this industry and I promised myself I would never take the piss when I became an employer.

Seven three-hour shifts work out at almost two hundred pounds. I take out the full two hundred in a mixture of tens and twenties – which I'm dismayed to see almost empties the till – and walk back around the front of the bar.

"Here you go," I say, handing the cash to Danielle. "And I'll make sure we sort it out with payroll before next time."

Her face lights up as she accepts the money and I shift my attention to her dad. The gesture has taken all the wind out of his sails. He mutters something under his breath, which I assume to be him saying a begrudging 'thank you', before he ushers his daughter off the stool and out of the restaurant.

I watch them leave and then return to the kitchen and join Pearl at the pass.

"How's it going, Chef?" I ask her.

She looks at me with arched eyebrows. Her cheeks are flushed and there are beads of sweat on her forehead, but I've never seen her look so invigorated. "It's going well. I think so. You picked a mad night to leave me in charge though. We've had two parties of eight in. I've been doubling up doing the fish and two of the starters along-side running the pass."

"Shit. Yeah. I forgot. Sorry to dump it on you tonight. I

was doing something important. But I'm impressed, Chef. Really. You're doing awesome."

Lawrence shoves two plates in front of her, both containing steak au poivre with fondant potato and braised cavolo nero. They look good. She inspects them briefly and wipes away a rogue droplet of sauce before shouting 'service' and smacking her palm down on the bell at the front of the counter.

"I'm having fun, to be honest," she says as Simone appears and takes the plates. "It's hard work though."

"No one said this life wasn't." I rest my hand on her shoulder, but my attention is on the door to the staff room over her shoulder. "Listen, do you think you can handle the rest of service? I've still got a few things I need to sort out in the office."

She looks up at me and wipes the back of her hand across her brow. I can almost sense the nervous energy coming off her. "Yes. Sure. I think so. Thanks."

"No, thank you," I say, already walking to the door. "But give me a shout if you need me. I'm only through here."

"Yes, Chef!"

I give her a thumbs up over my shoulder and go through into my office. The light is still on from when I was last here. I close the door and sit at the desk. With so much on my mind, I'm almost paralysed but I manage to gather myself together enough to switch on the computer and look at Danielle's personnel file. Jessie set up the electronic HR database when she was still here, but I've not kept the records up to date. I scan the documents. There should be one called *New Starter Information* that contains an employee's bank details, which are then sent to our outsourced payroll company. But it's not there. That would explain why the poor kid didn't get paid this month. I'm no good at admin. Jessie always handled the backend stuff, and not for the first time I find myself feeling lost here without her. I stand and pull out the first drawer of the filing cabinet and pull out a blank form. I scribble on a Post-It note – to remind me to get Danielle to fill it in on her next shift – and place it on the edge of my desk.

Sitting back down, I let out a long sigh. It feels good and makes me realise I've not taken a full deep breath in a while. For the last few days, I've existed in fight or flight mode all the way. Inhaling short, sharp breaths as my body bristles with nerves and anxiety.

I'm about to switch off the computer but something else compels me to click on the BBC news sites and see if there have been any updates on the body in the reservoir. Thankfully, I don't find any. But the original article, along with the subsequent one describing how the person had likely drowned, are both on the first page of the site and this fact doesn't help my mood. I reread the first report and see there is a new section at the bottom of the page. It's just one extra paragraph, highlighted in bold text and requesting that people come forward if they were around Woodhead Reservoir in the summer of 2002 and remember seeing anything. That means they've dated the skeleton and have got the time of death pretty bang-on perfect. It's amazing what forensics can do these days. Amazing and worrying. I suppose it depends on where you stand on the matter.

I log out of the computer and power it down, waiting as the screen switches to black. It looks as if the police have got nowhere in their investigation and, whilst I'm pleased with that fact, I can't shake this uneasy feeling.

Dan worries me. He's unstable and a loose cannon. I take
the note out of my back pocket and open it out.

I KNOW WHAT YOU ARE

He was convincing enough when I confronted him
earlier but that doesn't mean he didn't send it. It could just
be that he's a good liar.

But if he did send it, why? If he really wants to *cleanse
his soul*, as he's stated, it could be a way of forcing my
hand. Trying to make me go to the police and confess my
sins. Or, as I'm beginning to suspect more and more, is
this him forcing my hand another way?

To say Dan is down on his luck would be a massive
understatement. Are all these things – him coming back
here, his apparent desire to own up to what we did, and
now this threatening note – an elaborate way of getting
money out of me? Is it his plan to blackmail me, make me
pay for his silence?

I reach for the recent bank and credit card statements
and glance over them. A sharp sneer curls my lip. I have a
couple of thousand saved in another account that was
supposed to be for a rainy day, and I guess they don't get
much rainier than this. But that's only going to take us so
far. I screw the statements up into a ball and aim it at the
waste bin in the corner. If I get it in, then everything will
be all right, I tell myself. Holding my breath I make the
throw, not daring to move as the ball arcs through the air.
It hits the rim of the bin and looks as if it might fall in but
then hits the rim again on its second descent and bounces
off onto the carpet. Missed. I let my shoulders sag. What
did I expect? I place my head on the desk and close my
eyes.

If Dan wants me to buy his silence, he might as well start talking to the police right now. Because I don't have any money to give him.

Give it another six months, I won't even have a restaurant.

14

T he next day, as a last grasp at normality, I set my alarm for 4:45 a.m. and head out for another early morning run. This way I'm back, showered and dressed, and ready to make breakfast when Fern and Jessie come downstairs an hour later. Jessie has been awake most of the night with Noah and I was going to let her sleep in.

"What's the point?" she says as I tell her this. "He'll only wake up and want me to feed him." She looks exhausted and like she's at the end of her rope. I know how she feels.

"Coffee?" I ask as she sits down at the table.

She nods. "Keep it coming."

"Yeah, I feel you." I fill the filter coffee jug at the tap and use it to fill up the machine.

"Can I have coffee, Daddy?" Fern calls over. Her shrill voice sounds cute even at this hour.

I turn from the machine to see her. She's kneeling up on her chair beaming at me.

"I don't think you need it, shorty," I tell her. "Are you looking forward to school today?"

"It's *pre-school*, Daddy."

"Yes... I know... It's just... Never mind." I catch Jessie's eye and grin, hoping for a silent exchange of solidarity. I get a half-smile back. "Are you sure you're okay?" I ask her.

"Yes!" she snaps. "I'm just worn out."

I turn back to the coffee machine and fill it with the usual four scoops of coffee and one for luck.

Ha! Luck!

That's a good one.

After switching it on I go over to the table and sit next to Fern, opposite Jessie. "What would everyone like to eat? Bacon? Sausages? Toast? Cereal?"

"I want toast!" Fern announces. "With honey, please, and cut in triangles."

"No problem. Jess?"

She shakes her head. "I'm not hungry."

"You need to eat something."

"I'll get something later."

"Fair enough."

I make five slices of toast in case Jessie changes her mind. I place Fern's quartered, triangular offerings on a small plate in front of her and place another plate containing the remaining slices in the middle of the table. I know from experience if I push Jessie to eat, she'll get mad. This way it's her choice if she takes a slice. I hope she does. She's already lost all her baby weight and in the morning sunlight coming through the kitchen window, her cheeks have a hollow quality.

I sit and am about to pick up a slice of toast to eat while I wait for the coffee jug to fill when my phone vibrates. I've left it on the counter but leaning back I can reach it.

"It's a bit early to call someone," Jessie says. "Who is it?"

"It's probably a spam email or an irrelevant news update," I say, but as I bring it in front of me, I see it is indeed a message. From Dan. I open it up and scan-read the text. It's brief. He says he's been thinking about things and would like to talk about how we move forward.

I'd bet any money this is him paving the way to ask me for money. After I got back from the restaurant last night, I spent a while poring over my accounts. Depending on how much he wants, I might be able to get something together. I reckon I'm good for about a five-grand loan from the bank. Anything higher than that and it's a problem. I could ask my dad, but I don't want it to have to come to that.

"Why are you turning your phone away from me?" Jessie asks.

I look at her. "I'm not," I say. But, as I look down, I realise I am. Whether it's a survival instinct or an old habit I can't shake, I'm not sure.

"Who is it, Rob?"

"No one. It's just Dan." I flash her the phone, long enough that she can see his name at the top of the screen but not enough she'd be able to read the content of the message.

"What does he want?"

"He wants to meet up. That's all." Fern is staring at me, listening to the conversation. I make a face at her and she laughs."

"I don't understand what he's doing coming back

here," Jessie asks. "Didn't you say his family had all moved away?"

"They have. But he's a bit messed up. I think his time in the army did his head in. He's had a hard time these last few years and I think he wanted to come back home and be in a familiar environment. Back to the place where he felt the safest."

I surprise myself at how plausible this explanation sounds but Jessie lets out a bitter laugh and doesn't seem convinced.

"Who are you talking about?" Fern asks, with a mouthful of toast.

"Daddy's old friend," I tell her. "Dan. Do you remember?"

"With the silly hair."

"That's right." I laugh. "I had Pearl run the pass last night," I tell Jessie, hoping to change the subject. "She did great."

"Great."

She sounds prickly but I pretend not to notice. "Yes. I think I'm going to be able to rely on her more going forward. Which is good for us, isn't it? We're full tonight so I need to cover the evening service, but I could stay at home today if you want and help out. We could go for lunch?"

"I want to go for lunch," Fern says.

"You'll be at school!"

"*Pre-school*, Daddy."

"Yes. Sorry." I turn to Jessie. "What do you think?" It looks to me like she could really do with some support, but I also have selfish reasons for the offer. If I'm here with her and Noah, I'll be suitably distracted and I won't have

time to think about Dan and the body in the water and all
the terrible things I've done.

My phone beeps again. Another message from Dan.
Jessie rolls her eyes. "No, it's fine. You're clearly needed
elsewhere."

"It's not like that," I say. "He's just a bit needy."

"Is he? Does he *need* you, Rob? What about your
family?"

I sit back, glancing between her and Fern. I really
don't want to have this conversation in front of my daughter. I really don't want to be having this conversation at all!

"Where is this coming from?" I say, keeping my voice
low. "You know everything I do is for you and the kids. For
us. Work is hard at the moment but I'm doing all I can. I
want to spend more time at home with you all."

She sighs. "Fine."

I inhale sharply through my nose and lower my hands
into my lap so Fern can't see me balling them into fists. I
would never hit Jessie – or anyone. The frustration and rage
I feel are aimed inwards, but I need a release of some kind.

"What time does Fern need to be at sch— at pre-
school?"

"Quarter to nine."

I look at my phone screen. It's just gone eight. "I'll take
her. Are you ready, squirt?"

Fern scrunches up her face. "I need a poo."

"Of course you do," I sigh, and finally receive a flicker
of solidarity as Jessie catches my gaze. Just about, anyway.
I wink at her. "Right. Come with me, Ferny. We'll sort you
out and then get going. That'll give Mummy a bit of time
on her own before your brother wakes up."

Or at least, that was the idea. But as I bundle Fern out

of the house and shut the front door behind us, I hear Noah's cries drifting down from upstairs. Poor Jessie.

After dropping Fern off at pre-school, I give Jess a call, but she doesn't pick up. I leave a message instead, informing her that I'm going to go into the restaurant and asking her to call if she needs me, that I'd come home straight away. Once done I feel a bit better and drive to the restaurant with the stereo on loud and Tom Waits' raggedy voice spurring me on.

It's still early and I'm the first one there so I open up and even unstack both industrial dishwashers from the night before. Once done, I go through into the office and check the rota. Danielle is working the lunch service, so I take the form out into the bar area and place it there with a note attached for her or Simone to see. If I get it to payroll today, then she'll be on the list for the next payday. I'm feeling rather pleased with myself as I sit back down behind my desk. I'm not usually this organised and future-focused, but I know from experience that when I am, everything flows easier and is a lot less stressful. I vow to remain this way going forward, and not just at work.

How we do anything is how we do everything.

It's a few minutes after ten when the office phone goes. These days, most orders and bookings are done online, so it's not rung for days and when it does it makes me jump. I compose myself and lift the receiver.

"Good morning, Fire and Ice Restaurant, Rob Wilkes speaking."

The person on the other end doesn't respond.

"Hello?" I say. "Fire and Ice. Who's there, please?" I wait a few seconds. "I'm sorry, I can't hear you. Are you there?"

I listen. There is no background noise. No wind or cars

or even any static on the line. But then I hear something like a low wheezing sound. Breathing.

"Who is this?" I ask.

There's no answer. I hang the phone up but hold onto the receiver, staring at it as I try to work out what'd just happened. Being out in the sticks, people's mobile phone reception is sometimes iffy but it didn't sound like that was what was going on. I'm aware I'm seeing the world via a frame of stress and paranoia right now but, nevertheless, it sounded like a prank call.

Dan.

It has to be.

I pick the receiver up again but get the dialling tone. I dial the number that tells you the last caller's number but, of course, it was withheld.

"Bloody idiot," I mutter, placing the phone down and getting up from my desk. But I've no time to worry about his silly games right now. As I walk through into the kitchen I find Pearl and Tony washing down ready for lunchtime. It's time to go to work.

THE NEXT FEW hours fly by. The kitchen is a pulsating beast of activity, and I don't stop once, getting stuck in wherever I can.

Busy hands – quiet mind.

After helping Lawrence prep a large bowl of Jerusalem artichokes for today's risotto I join Pearl over by the fish counter and shuck a bag of fresh oysters ready for the evening menu. They look great, and for the first time in a while, I feel excited about the dishes we're creating here at Fire and Ice. Owning my own restaurant has been my dream for so long, yet with all the stress of the pandemic so soon after we opened and then Jessie getting pregnant, I've not really had the chance to appreciate it.

But I did it.

I've done it.

I am the owner of a fine-dining restaurant and I need to keep in mind how lucky I am. I'm not one of those happy-clappy souls who believe being grateful for every little thing is somehow a magical pathway to success. But right now, I'll try anything I can to keep my head above water and the lights on.

Lunchtime rolls around and we're busier than I expected, which is a bonus and also means I feel vindicated I came to work rather than staying at home. I also know Jessie does get to catch up on her sleep in the daytime when Noah is napping, so I'd only disturb her if I was pottering around.

I'm plating up a steak frites special when I hear the phone in my office ringing for the second time today. And just like that, all the good energy I've been amassing over the last few hours drains out of me.

It's another prank call. I can feel it in my bones.

I slide the finished dish onto the pass and ring the bell for service before marching through the staff room and into the office. Shaking my head to try and remove the bad thoughts already forming, I grab hold of the receiver and hold it to my ear.

"Good afternoon, Fire and Ice Restaurant. Rob Wilkes speaking." My greeting is only a little curter than it was this morning but, when once again there's no answer, the anger quickly bubbles up inside of me. "Who is this? What the hell do you want?"

I pause. I can hear breathing for certain this time.

"Listen to me," I snarl through gritted teeth. "You need

to stop this; do you hear me? This isn't fair. I don't need this on top of everything else."

This time I hear an intake of breath. The bastard isn't even hiding it now. He's there on the other end. Listening but not speaking. Trying to scare me. I've had it. The rage that I've been fighting with for the past days bubbles up inside of me.

"You wanker!" I tell him. "What do you hope to achieve by doing this? Do you want to make me more fucked up than I already am? Because, if so – well done, you're managing it! Now just leave me alone! Do you hear me? Leave me the fuck alone or else!"

I slam the phone down but am startled by a sharp cough coming from behind me. I spin around to see Simone framed in the doorway. She looks me up and down with concerned eyes.

"What's going on, Rob?"

I hold up one finger and point to the phone but when no suitable words come to me, I use it to scratch my head. "Was I shouting?"

"Yes. We could all hear. Who was it?"

I close my eyes in a futile attempt to hide from the awkwardness filling me up. "Sorry, Simone. It was a prank caller. Kids, probably, being stupid. It's the second time today so..." I open my eyes, using them to plead with Simone for understanding.

She smiles at me the way Dad does sometimes. "Bloody kids."

"Yeah. I know. It's not what I need right now." I puff out my cheeks. "You were right the other day. I've not been sleeping well with Noah and... I guess I'm not dealing with things too well."

"Do you want to talk about it?"

"No. Thank you. I can cope."

She tilts her head to one side. "Are you sure? You do seem a bit... not yourself lately. It might be helpful."

"Thanks, I'll come and find you if I change my mind."

She folds her arms. "Well, you obviously need rest. Why don't you go home for a few hours before we open again? We've almost finished here now except for a few deserts and the checks. I can finish up."

I frown. "Are you sure? I don't want to put loads of work on—"

"Go home, Rob. You're no good to us all hyped up and stressed."

"Fair enough."

I thank her and change out of my whites before slipping out of the back door unseen by the rest of my team. I don't want to face anyone presently. But as I get in the van and drive out of the car park to the end of the road, I take a left onto the high street rather than turn right for home.

I drive up past the train station and take a left down the side of Manor Park. I've no idea where I'm heading. I just want to drive. To get out of my head for a while. I switch on the stereo to hear Tom still doing his thing. It's not what I need right now. I skip it to the next CD already loaded in the player and get Nick Cave's *The Boatman's Call*. It's another classic but I need something faster and heavier. Something with more bite. On the third skip, I get *Appetite for Destruction* by Guns N' Roses. Perfect. I drive on as the opening bars of *Paradise City* blast in my ears.

I drive all the way down Manor Park Road and take a left by The Bull's Head, following the road until it comes out on Woodhead Road. Up to this point, my path has been clear but the winding nature of these roads and the parked cars means I haven't been able to go fast. I want to go fast. I take a right, accelerating up the hill, past the garden centre and then put my foot down as the road levels off. As *It's So Easy* comes on the stereo I watch the speedometer rise from forty to fifty to sixty. The roads here are still winding and narrow but I don't care, taking the bends without slowing down. I'm being reckless, I know I am. And I'm also aware of the bitter irony of me driving so irresponsibly – given the reason why I need this release today. But, still, I don't care. A searing rage competes with confusion and fear in my system, and I don't want to feel any of those things.

I don't want to feel anything.

I drive as far as Glossop Sailing Club and then a large truck coming the other way means I have to slow down. I use the club's car park to turn around and head back the way I've come, this time taking a left by the garden centre and driving through Little Padfield.

From here, I'm not too far away from Dad's place and before I know it, I'm parked up outside the end terrace where I grew up and where he still lives. I switch off the engine but don't get out straight away. Instead, I sit and watch the house, searching for signs of movement through the large bay window. I'm not sure what I'm waiting for. I wonder if maybe I want him to see me sitting here so he'll beckon me inside and the decision to talk to him will be taken out of my hands. I know if I did open up to him – about the restaurant, about Jessie, even about Dan – that he'd understand. Or if he didn't understand, he'd try to. My dad is a clever man and has been so empathetic and kind to me over the years. Often when I didn't deserve it. I'm his only child and he loves me, but it's deeper than that. He's my rock and I know I can rely on him. It was his influence, I think, that gave me the courage and strength of mind to move to London when I couldn't cope with life up here any longer. He was sad about me going, especially as mum hadn't long passed, but he helped me move all the same and drove me down there in his friend's van. He's a great man. He's an even better dad.

So, why can't I face him?

Is it guilt which is holding me back from speaking to him? Fear? The dashboard clock reads 3:17 p.m. I give it until 3:20 p.m. and when he still hasn't appeared at the window, I start the car and drive away.

I pull into my drive fifteen minutes later and get out.

I can tell immediately something's wrong. It's as if my senses are picking up on clues my logical brain hasn't yet noticed. I crunch across the gravel pathway up to the front door and that's when I see it. A dead crow, lying on the doorstep.

"What the—"

I spin around so fast I almost stumble over. Steadying myself by holding onto the side of the house I scan the area, searching the fields and trees beyond our walls for a sign of who left this here. Because someone did leave it. I'm sure of that fact.

"Hello?" I call out. "Dan?"

No one answers and there's no one in sight. I still have my keys in my hand, and I use the remote control to open the door of the adjoining garage. I enter as soon at its viable, hunkering down under the slow-moving door to get inside quickly. I head to the back wall and grab the old spade that once belonged to my grandad before marching back outside. I scoop up the dead bird on the spade and carry it over to the wall that runs around the perimeter of our lot and fling the carcass into the neighbouring field. I imagine a cat or a fox will have it for dinner later.

As I get back to the front door, I see there's blood on the step and a pile of black feathers. The scene looks even creepier if anything, but the hose pipe makes short work of the mess and once I'm finished, you'd never know anything was here.

But I know.

My heart is going like the clappers as I unlock the front door and go inside.

"Jess," I call out. "It's me."

There's no answer. I go into the kitchen. She's not there.

"Jessie," I shout, louder. "Where are you?"

I go to the bottom of the stairs but can't hear anything. The house feels empty, the air devoid of energy. Grabbing the handrail, I haul myself up to the landing and put my head around the door of Fern's room then go into ours. She's not here. I go over to Noah's crib that we've set up near the wall on her side of the bed. It's empty.

"Jessie?"

She always tells me when she's going out. Especially since Noah was born. She feels it's important that I know. I check my phone. No messages. No missed calls.

So, where the hell is she?

With my imagination taking me into dark and uncomfortable places, I run back downstairs and do another lap of the kitchen and lounge before heading outside. I walk down the drive and cross the road to our nearest neighbours, the Johnsons. They've lived around here forever and, both being in their early seventies, are at home most days. They keep themselves to themselves but are a pleasant enough couple. When Jessie and I were both working at the restaurant they'd often take delivery of parcels we had sent to the house without any bother.

I knock on their front door, resisting the urge to slam my fist against the wood with more urgency when it's not opened straight away. I hear movement and a key in a lock and then Mr Johnson – Geoff– puts his face around the side of the door.

"Hello, Rob."

"Have you seen anyone lurking around my house at all?" I say, but it's now that I realise how out of breath I am. I gulp back a mouthful of air and try to compose myself. "Sorry, Geoff. I just got home and there was a..." I pause, suddenly feeling rather silly. Is this me being paranoid? The crow could have flown into one of the upstairs windows and broken its neck. It happens. But, no. It's too much of a coincidence. I look up at Geoff's confused expression. "I think someone's been trespassing in my garden," I say. "Did you see anyone?"

He cranes his neck to peer over the road at our house. "No, I'm sorry. I've not seen anything out of the ordinary."

"Right. Okay." I'm about to leave but I turn back. "You didn't see Jessie leaving with anyone?"

He shakes his head. "We've been engrossed in Countdown for the last hour, I'm afraid. It's a good one today." His eyes light up as if he's about to give me a full rundown of the quiz show episode he's just watched.

"No worries, Jack. Thanks anyway. Sorry to bother you." I smile and back away before running all the way back to my house.

I can feel a tightness in my chest and my head feels as if it's in a vice. It's not a headache as much as a gripping pain. As if every muscle in my face has turned to stone. If Dan was behind the prank calls and the dead crow, he's more unstable and dangerous than I thought. I have to put an end to this. I have to get him out of our lives.

"Jessie!" I shout as I get into the house. I go through into the kitchen and spin around like a whirling dervish. I've no idea what to do.

Where the hell are my wife and baby son?

She has been acting rather erratically lately. She's not been herself. But she wouldn't leave without telling me. Would she? Oh God, what if she's—?

No! Don't be ridiculous!

More paranoid thoughts swirl around my brain. I know she's been struggling a bit with her mental health since Noah was born but that's just the baby blues, as they call it. It's not nice, but she seems on top of it.

And she would never do anything to put her children in danger.

So where is she? Where's Noah? Where's Fern, come to think of it?

Oh no! Fern.

Shit!

I glance at the clock above the oven. It's 3:50 p.m. I was supposed to text her and let her know if I could pick Fern up from pre-school. When it got to 3:30 p.m. and she hadn't heard from me she must have set off herself with Noah in the pram. The fact she didn't tell me this is more likely a sign she's pissed off with me rather than anything sinister.

As if to put a final, glorious end to this waking anxiety dream of my own making, I hear Fern's laughter drifting in through the front door. I've left it open, which will probably annoy Jessie, too. But they're home.

Thank God!

"Daddy!" Fern yells, running into the kitchen. I kneel and she leaps into my arms. "I missed you today."

"Aww, darling. I missed you, too," I tell her. "Did you have a good day?"

She nods. "I did you a picture. And one for Mummy. Now I'm home I'm going to do one for your friend."

I lean back so I can look at her. My mouth is dry when I ask, "Which friend?"

"Your friend with the silly hair. Look, he's come to see you."

A movement to my right catches my attention and I look up to see Dan standing in the doorway. He grins at me and looks down at my baby son, who's asleep in his arms.

"Hey, mate," he says. "Are you putting the kettle on?"

15

I stand and stare at Dan, hesitant as to what to say to him. Jessie appears in the hallway behind him and greets me with an austere expression on her face.

"Look who we bumped into on the walk back from school," she says, moving past him and holding my gaze, letting me know how unhappy she is about this development.

"Ah, I see. Bumped into him, did you?" But the question is directed at Dan.

Jessie dumps her bag on the table and takes her coat off before retrieving Noah from Dan's clutches. Once she's got him safely in her arms, I allow my shoulders to relax a touch.

"I thought it'd be nice," Dan says, stepping into the kitchen and looking around. "Are you making a pot of tea, then?'

I mutter something under my breath that is more noise than words and walk over and fill the kettle from the tap. Behind me, I hear Jessie corralling Fern out of the kitchen and upstairs to get changed. I wait until I hear the creak of the landing floorboards before I speak.

"What the fuck are you playing at?"

Dan doesn't answer so I turn around.

"What do you mean?" he asks when I do.

I take the kettle over to its power point and switch it on before walking up to him. "Was it you? Today on the phone?" I'm speaking in hushed tones, and it makes me sound more threatening than I intend. I think about stepping back. If Dan is as unstable as I believe him to be, I don't want to push him over the edge. Not in my house, at least. Not in front of my kids. But I also want him to know I'm not messing around. "It stops, Dan. Now."

His confused expression twists into a smirk. "What are you talking about?"

"You know full well what I'm talking about. And the dead crow, too? Nice touch. I'll be honest, that freaked me out but—"

"Whoa! Robby!" He holds his hands up. "I've no idea what the hell you're going on about."

"Don't you?" I stare deep into his eyes but don't really know what I'm looking for. "What do you want?" I ask him.

"Tea. Two sugars." He grins.

"You're a dick, do you know that? This is not fair. I've got a family. I've got people who rely on me. Why are you doing this?"

"Doing what?" He scoffs and I want to punch him so much that I have to walk away. I go to the cupboard and take down three mugs and place them next to the boiling kettle.

"Is it money?" I ask, dragging the box of tea bags across the counter and taking out three. He doesn't answer so I try again. "Are you here because you think you can get money out of me? Is that it, Dan? Are you trying to black-mail me?"

"What the fuck?" he says, dragging each word out as far as each syllable can reasonably go. "Is that what you think of me?"

"I don't know you, Dan." The kettle boils and I fill the cups, using the time to try to arrange my thoughts into a coherent thread. Dan is bad news. I know that for sure. I have to get him out of my home and out of my life for good.

"I came back to Glossop because I wanted to put some demons to bed," he says. "When I saw the news about the body in the water everything came flooding back to me. What I did. What we did. I realised that this was the point when my life took a bad turn." He laughs to himself. "Do you know what my therapist told me once – the guy who diagnosed me with PTSD? He said it was understandable being in a high-pressure situation where I had to kill people that it would have a negative effect on me." I catch his eye and he sneers. "I know, right? These people get paid a shit-tonne of cash to state the bleeding obvious. But you see, the more I thought about it I realised it was more than that. What we did profoundly affected me. It changed who I was and how I thought about myself."

It's my turn to scoff. "Yes. It did to me as well. We've both had our crosses to bear, mate. My life isn't all sunshine and rainbows, believe me." As I say this my eyes fall on one of Fern's drawings stuck to the fridge. It's a drawing of a sun and some rainbows. The sun looks to be smiling at me and normally that would cheer me up. Today, the representation of my daughter's innocence only makes me feel sick.

"You seem to be doing well," Dan says.

"It might look that way from the outside." I turn my attention back to the drinks, mashing each teabag against the side of the mug and chucking them in the bowl we use for such things. I finish off with milk and sugar for Dan and hand him the mug.

He sips at it and makes a satisfied noise as I walk around the table and sit so I'm facing him.

"Whatever you're doing, whatever it is you have planned, it has to stop. I mean it. I will not let you ruin my life."

He places his hand on his chest. "I don't want to do that. Why would you say that?"

"Because," I yell, then catch myself and lower my voice. "Because you're talking about going to the police and telling them what we did."

He holds my gaze and doesn't blink. "I keep telling you, I need to cleanse my soul."

"Yes. I know. But what the hell does that even mean?"

He sips at his tea and does a good impression of a hammy actor coming to terms with a difficult decision. "I just don't know what to do for the best," he says.

I hate him in that moment. I don't know why we were ever friends.

"It's not my fault your life didn't turn out the way you wanted it to," I say, getting up from the table.

"Isn't it?"

"You think it is?"

He shrugs. "Who knows." He smacks his lips and hands me the mug. "I'd better get off anyway, leave you people to get settled in for the night."

"Don't do anything stupid, Dan. Please."

He winks. "I won't. Not yet anyway."

"How much longer are you staying for?"

He goes to the door and stops. "I don't know, mate," he says. "A few more days, a week, forever. It all depends."

"On what?"

He twists his mouth to one side. "I'm not sure." Then he gives me a sharp salute and disappears into the hallway. "See you later, mate," he calls back as he leaves.

LATER THAT NIGHT, after the kids are asleep and we've had dinner, Jessie and I sit on the sofa together. Together, but alone. Neither of us speaks but I can sense tension coming from Jessie. She's been like this ever since Dan left.

Did she hear us? And if so, what was said? I replay the events of a few hours earlier. I can't remember whether I said anything incriminating and that worries me.

Maybe I should come clean to her. Maybe it's time. She is my wife and she's evidently picked up on the fact that I'm acting weirder than usual. I've got to tell her something.

"Sorry about Dan turning up like that," I try.

She doesn't reply straight away but then she twists in her seat and her face is already creased into an angry frown. "What the fuck is his problem?" she snaps. "Inviting himself back here and strutting around like he owns the place. You know he never looks me in the eye whenever he speaks to me. Not once. I don't think he likes me. And what was going on between the two of you? It was odd."

I blink to rouse myself. It seems she's been stewing on this a while. I adjust my position on the sofa so we're face to face.

"Was it odd? I didn't notice."

"Really? What's he doing here, sniffing around? I know he's supposed to be your old mate or whatever but I've never heard you mention him in ten years. I've never seen any old photos of him, he didn't come to the wedding. You can't have been that close."

"It was a long time ago."

"What was?"

I baulk at her question. "When we were friends."

"Is that all you were?"

"What do you mean?"

She shrugs and curls her lip. "I don't know. Was he your wingman? When you were out screwing a different woman every night? Or was it more than that? Maybe he joined in."

"Bloody hell! Come on, Jessie, we've had this conversation too many times now. All that was before I met you. You changed me for the better. I love you. You don't have to worry about it. Or even think about it. That's not who I am anymore."

"You're still keeping things from me. I know you're lying to me."

"I'm not! I never lied to you."

"Yes! You did!"

"I chose not to tell you something straight away because I didn't want to fuck things up between us. I would have told you eventually. Not telling someone something isn't lying."

"It is, Rob! It is to me!"

"I'm not lying to you. You're being stupid." I stop myself as soon as I hear it and suck air through my teeth. "Sorry, Jess. I didn't mean that. All I'm doing is trying to keep this family afloat and look after you and the kids.

Right now, I feel like I'm on a hamster wheel and I can't get off."

Jessie snorts. "Oh, I'm so sorry. Whereas I'm just sitting here all day on my arse doing nothing."

I turn away from her intense stare before it turns me to stone. How did we get back onto this? I wanted to lean into her just now, tell her what was going on. Part of it at least.

"I didn't mean you weren't struggling too, Jess," I say. "I just mean that... Ah, bollocks. I don't know what I mean. I don't even know what I'm trying to say anymore. Everything has turned very confusing and scary all of a sudden."

"What has?"

"*Everything*?"

"Us?"

This is the last thing I need right now. My body is tingling with internalised anger and I don't know how to release it.

"No. Not us."

"You told me there were no more secrets. You promised me. That night in that hotel, when it all came out, about you being more prolific in the womanising stakes than Russell fucking Brand – you swore to me there were no more surprises. But there is, Rob. You and Dan. Something is going on. I don't know what it is, but you're up to something. Why won't you tell me?"

I rub my eyes. "There isn't anything. It's just... He's not very well. Mentally. Emotionally. Being in Afghanistan messed his head up but he doesn't like people to know. That's all it is."

Why?

Why am I saying this to her?

I'm only digging a bigger hole for myself!

"He's a bit down on his luck, that's all," I go on. "I feel sorry for him."

"Is he after money?"

The bluntness of her question and the fact she's immediately drilled into the notion that's been swirling around in the peripheries of my thoughts for the last few days floors me. I open my mouth to respond but shut it again.

She glares at me. "Well?"

"I think he'd appreciate some financial help."

"And you're going to give it him? Why?"

I lean back. "I didn't say that. We don't... We can't... I mean, it's mostly tied up in the business, and anyway, I think—"

"I knew you'd do something like this eventually," she hisses. It comes out of nowhere and I've no idea how to respond. "I knew it. You're all the same." She gets to her feet.

"I'm not like...*them.*" I say, meaning her exes. "Where are you going? And what do you mean, *I'd do something like this*? Like what?"

"You know. Ruin things. Ruin us."

"Is that what you think I'm doing?"

"Don't you?"

"No!" She turns to leave but I grab her shoulder. "Jessie, talk to me."

"Get off of me." She shakes my hand away and shoves me in the chest. It's not hard but the shock of it hurts. "Go to hell."

"Jesus! I don't need this on top of everything else!" I step towards her, and she raises her hand. She looks as if she's about to swipe it across my face, but she doesn't.

Instead, she looks away and bursts into tears. That's worse.

"Please can you sleep on the sofa tonight."

I move around the side of her to try and make eye contact but she won't look at me. "Fine. I will."

"Thanks. There are spare covers in the utility room." She turns and walks out of the room. I stand there for a moment before sitting back on the sofa.

What the hell just happened?

Did I cause this?

Was this my fault?

I sit back and rest my head against the back of the sofa cushion. What a bloody mess I've made of things. But I'm going to fix it. All of it.

I have to.

16

The sofa is uncomfortable and lumpy, and I hardly sleep a wink. At 5 a.m. I get up and tiptoe into mine and Jessie's bedroom and grab my running gear. My hope is a few kilometres will clear my head but it's a misty morning despite being warm and I end up coughing my lungs up at the top of Primrose Lane. I walk most of the way home, feeling more defeated than when I set off.

Jessie and the kids are up and eating breakfast when I get back. I say hello to Fern and give Noah a cuddle, but Jessie doesn't look at me. Usually, it's me who stews on things. I can hold a grudge for days, whereas Jessie blows up fast but forgets about it almost immediately. I'm not sure which is best for your soul or peace of mind but today I wish she was more like she used to be. I want the old Jessie back. I want to forget we argued and go back to normal.

But then, I want to forget a lot of things.

I also wish I could stay at home and sort things out with her but it's almost the weekend and I've got a delivery of fresh halibut and seabream arriving first thing, and I need to be at the restaurant to sign for it.

When I tell her this it's met with vague acknowledgement and a sense of the inevitable from Jessie. It feels as if she's accusing me of not caring as she tells me, "That's fine," and that I should, "Do what you need to do."

Her eyes are red and puffy but from what I remember of last night Noah only woke up once. She should have had a decent night's sleep.

Should have...

I arrive at the restaurant at 9:15 a.m. and only get a chance to unlock the back door before the beep of a horn announces Andrew Marsden's arrival with the fish.

"Where do you want it, squire?" he bellows in his customary cockney accent as he brings the first tray up the back steps and into the kitchen. "There're some lovely beasts in here this week. Fat as ya like and it just flakes off the bone. Lovely stuff."

Yes, and the cost highlights that, I think to myself, as he hands me the delivery receipt and invoice.

I get him to put the three trays of fresh fish into the refrigerator unit and, once he's done, I thank him with a firm shake of the hand. His are freezing cold and rather slimy. After he leaves, I hold my hand up to my nose and am repulsed by the stench of fish this early in the morning.

Due to the atmosphere in the kitchen, I didn't eat breakfast, which hasn't helped. I wash my hands liberally in the sink and go into the larder to see if there's any spare morsel that I can stuff in my face to keep me going. Whilst I'm in there, pressing my thumb into one of last night's bread rolls to assess its edibleness, I hear the front door of the restaurant go and the sound of letters falling onto the mat. More bills, I imagine.

I chuck the bread roll in the bin and go through into the main dining area. The mail has scattered itself across the floor and, as I approach, I can see at least three thin brown envelopes that are most likely going to send me under a dark cloud once I open them. But there's another envelope in the mix. A white one that's a different shape and size from the others. It looks like the sort of envelope which might contain a birthday card. Or a threatening note.

Not another.

I told him to stop. I was adamant. I thought he might have listened.

After scooping up all the envelopes, I shuffle the white one to the top. This one has a stamp on it and is addressed to me, at the restaurant. I narrow my eyes at the words on the front. It's handwritten in block capital letters and done in blue ballpoint pen. It also looks vaguely familiar, but I realise the thin, spidery letter shapes remind me of the way my mum used to write when she wasn't well. It's the erratic writing of someone rather troubled.

I rip it open. Even though I know what's inside and who sent it and why my hands are shaking as I remove the contents and open it out. This time there are just two words on the paper.

OWN UP!

It's done in the same cut-out style as the first one, and I notice in passing that the exclamation mark is actually an upside-down 'i'. I don't know why that troubles me so much, but it does.

Still staring at the note, I walk it back into the kitchen
and through into my office. I place the paper down on the
desk and am about to sit when I see another white envelope. Someone has rested it on the computer keyboard,
propped up in between the top and middle rows of keys.
There is no address on this one, just my name written in
the same spidery capital letters.

I pick it up. Where did this one come from? Instinct
has me turning around and walking back into the kitchen
as if I might find the answers there. But there is nothing. I
lean against the chrome countertop and tear open the
envelope. This note is longer, so the letters chosen are
smaller and not all of them are capitals.

It'S over. YOu'vE rUN oUt of lUCK. TruTH! NoW!

I crumple the paper in my fist and stuff it in the food
bin in the corner of the room, covering the evidence with
a handful of celeriac peelings.

This is getting too heavy. It has to stop. Right now. But
how do I go about stopping it? I've already had it out with
Dan and he acts as if he's completely innocent and doesn't
know what I'm talking about. I wish I knew what he was
thinking, what his agenda was. I appreciate he's having a
shitty time of it and he thinks my life is great compared to
his, but that's not a reason to ruin my life. He's unhinged
and unreasonable and bitter.

How do you reason with someone like that?

The thought crosses my mind that I should call his
bluff. I'll go to the police. I'll tell them we're both guilty of
death by dangerous driving and covering up an accident –
or whatever the technical terms for our crimes are. I'll tell
them the body they found in the dried-up reservoir is a

poor old man we knocked down twenty years ago when we were drunk.

Let's see how you like that, Dan. If the army was bad, how about prison? How about we both go down for this?

But that's now what you want, really, isn't it, old chum?

What you want is to make me pay for something you think I've done. Which is – what? – having a nice life when you couldn't?

And yes, I'm being flippant. But a part of me wonders if it is time for me to go to the police. I can't live like this. Dan is becoming more of a threat – and not only to my sanity but my life and livelihood too. He's crazy. My family could be in danger.

As my train of thought continues down this path, something else hits me. Something I've not even considered up to now. It stops me in my tracks and prickles all the hairs on the back of my neck.

What if it isn't Dan sending the notes?

I scratch at the two days' worth of stubble on my chin. If it's not him sending them, it means someone else knows what we did. Someone was there that night. I close my eyes, willing myself to remember. Could there have been another car further up the road? Or maybe one of the cottages up on the hillside had a clearer viewpoint down to the road than I've realised up to now. I don't think that could be the case. But, right now, I'm trusting my judgement on things less and less. Forget Dan being crazy, I feel as if I'm losing my mind.

I need to speak with him and have it out once and for all. If I have to throw money at him to get him out of my life, then I'll find a way. I'll beg, steal or borrow if I have to.

I tap the pockets of my jeans. Where the hell did I put my phone? I go into the staff room and rifle through my jacket but it's not there either. Grinding my teeth together, I replay the past hour. I had it in the kitchen at home. Is it still there? By the kettle? Shit. With all the stress and upset this morning I must have left without it.

But I need to speak to Dan before I lose my nerve. I grab my jacket and head for the door.

It takes me less than ten minutes to drive home, and when I get in Jessie is sitting at the kitchen table cradling Noah. He's crying. So is she. But rather than trying to comfort him, she's just staring out the window.

"Jessie," I say, placing my hands on the tabletop and tilting my head to try to make eye contact. "Has something happened? Something else?"

She doesn't move. "I'm fine," she says, in a monotonous tone.

She seems to be struggling more than usual. I wonder if I should sit with her and talk through what she said last night, about me ruining things, but I'm hoping I can put her outburst down to tiredness and new-baby hormones. Besides, all my energy is focused on speaking with Dan. Once I've done that, and I know he's taken care of, she'll have my full attention. I glance over at the kettle. My phone is lying beside it, as I thought.

"It's been ringing," Jessie says.

I look back at her but she's still staring out the window. Noah's screaming seems to be getting worse. I wonder if I should take him off her and try to comfort him. I hover over the table for a few seconds and bounce from foot to foot in the most awkward of dances before going to my phone.

"I'm so sorry," I say. "I need to make a really important phone call and then I swear I'll take him off you for an hour or so. You can have a nap or a bath. Yeah?" I nod and smile as eagerly as I can, hoping some of the positivity will rub off on her. But she doesn't answer.

I lift my phone and open the screen. There are three missed calls, all from a number I don't recognise, and each one is five minutes apart. It's probably a spam call, I tell myself as I scroll through my recent calls list to find Dan's number. I'm about to tap the call button when a loud knocking on the front door stops me.

"Are you expecting anyone?" I ask Jessie.

She shrugs. "Postman?"

I place my phone down and walk through into the hall. On the other side of the front door's frosted glass, I can see two dark silhouettes. My heart is already pounding as I open the door to reveal two men, both dressed in dark blue overcoats. I know straight away who they are. Or, at least, what they are.

"Robert Wilkes?" one of them says.

"That's me."

He nods. "I'm DCI Finlay and this is my colleague, DCI Wetherby. I wonder if we might come in?"

I lead the two police officers through into the kitchen. Jessie is now nowhere to be seen, which I find rather odd. I don't have time to linger on this thought, however, as DCI Finlay and DCI Wetherby enter the room and look around.

"Lovely place," Finlay says. He's the older of the two of them, with thinning orange hair and a freckled complexion. "It must be lovely and quiet up here, away from the town."

"It has its moments," I reply.

"How long have you lived here?" DCI Wetherby asks, still examining the space. With his thick black hair and dark skin, he looks to be mixed race, or maybe of Spanish origin; it's hard to tell.

"In this house, a few years," I say. "Before that, we lived in London. But I'm from the area originally. My dad has lived in Hadfield all his life."

Wetherby gives me a knowing smile. "So, you were around in the summer of 2002?"

"Yes, I think so. I mean, yes, I was." The question has unsettled me, and I go over to the kettle in case it shows on my face. I flick it on. "Would you like a drink?"

Wetherby looks as if he's about to reply in the affirmative, but Finlay holds his hand up. "Not for us, thank you, sir. We won't keep you long."

"Fair enough. What's this about?"

Shit.

I should have asked that as soon as they walked in.

Now they'll suspect I know exactly why they're here.

"I believe you know Daniel Chapman. You're old friends, he said."

I gnaw on my bottom lip with my top teeth as I consider how to answer. "Yep. I know Dan. We grew up together."

"Yes, that's what he said. May I...?" DCI Finlay pulls out one of the chairs.

"Sure, have a seat."

He sits and makes a show of getting comfortable before he continues. I can't tell whether he's being fussy or trying to freak me out.

"You might have seen the unit we've set up in the square," he goes on. "We're gathering any information we can regarding the human remains found in the reservoir recently. I suspect you've also heard about that?"

I nod, working on keeping my expression neutral. "Yes. How awful."

DCI Wetherby sits as well. The difference in levels – with me standing and them sitting – makes me uncomfortable. I feel as if I'm on stage being watched.

"Mr Chapman called into the unit this morning," Wetherby says. "He spoke to one of our colleagues and once he'd told them what was on his mind, they rang us so we could have a chat with him also. I understand he's just returned to the area."

"That's right. We've recently found each other," I say. "After a long time. It's nice to have him back."

"Hmm. Yes," Wetherby says, leaving me fretful. "Now, in terms of the skeleton that was found, we've got a ballpark figure on time of death being sometime in the summer of 2002. Mr Chapman told us you and he would often drive along the road to Holmfirth late at night that summer. Is that true?"

I scowl, hoping it looks like I'm trying to think. My brain is going into overdrive. Dark thoughts and paranoid ideas swirl around in my head.

Is this it? Has Dan confessed all? Are these police officers playing with me, providing me with enough rope to hang myself?"

"We used to go to a folk night over in Holmfirth," I say. "And there were no buses or anything, so we'd take it in turns to drive there and back. Whoever was driving didn't drink, of course."

"Of course," Finlay repeats and gives me a condescending smile. "Glad to hear it, Mr Wilkes."

I smile back at him but his face has turned stern. I want to run away. I want to cry. I pull in a deep breath. Maybe it's time to give up my secrets. They do say that when you reach rock bottom, it can be a relief. When there's nowhere left to fall, the only way is up.

I clear my throat, readying myself to confess everything. I'll tell them that I was lying just now, and Dan and I were actually both very drunk one night. I'll explain how Dan wasn't looking where he was going and he ended up knocking an old man down. A realisation buoys me. The fact Dan was driving might make me only an accessory to the crime. Is that how it works? Is that better for me?

No, idiot. Of course it isn't.

You still threw the poor old bugger into the water.

You still filled his pockets with rocks.

"Mr Chapman recalls seeing something on the side of the road one evening and remembers thinking it was a dead sheep," DCI Wetherby says. "He also noted it was unusual to see one on that road so late at night."

I close my mouth as a ripple of nervous energy pulses down my throat. It sounds as if Dan hasn't confessed after all.

So why the hell has he spoken to the police?

But I know the answer to that, don't I? This is for my benefit. It's another threat. A warning to me that I should do what he says – or else.

"Mr Chapman wonders now if perhaps it might have been the poor soul who eventually ended up in the water," DCI Finlay butts in.

"I see," I shake my head. "I'm sorry but I can't remember seeing anything. If it was a sheep, I probably didn't take it in. Especially if it was Dan driving that night."

I feel rather pleased with myself for adding this last part. Let's see how that prick likes being implicated.

Finlay sits back and folds his arms. "I'll be honest with

you, Mr Wilkes, we've not had many leads regarding this case so we're jumping on anything we can right now. We appreciate this might be nothing at all. But any information you can offer us is helpful."

I sense my heart rate returning to normal. "I wish I could be more help," I tell him. "It was a very long time ago but I'm sure if I had seen anything untoward, or of note, I'd remember it. But I'm sorry. I don't."

I look between the two police officers with my mouth fixed in a sympathetic smile. They glance at each other and Finlay sighs and gets to his feet.

"Thank you anyway, Mr Wilkes," he says. "We'll get out of your hair."

"If you do think of anything," Wetherby adds, taking a card from his pocket and handing it to me, "please give me a call."

I wave the card at him. "Absolutely."

The two men nod and head for the door but before he gets there, Finlay stops and turns around. "Just one thing," he says like he's bloody Columbo. "Mr Chapman said he only returned to the area very recently. Do you know why he came back? I thought my colleague had taken a statement before we arrived at the unit, but apparently not."

"Oh? I'm not sure. I did ask but he was sort of vague." I lower my voice in a conspiring way. "Between me and you, I don't think he's been doing great recently. He was in the army. Afghanistan. I think he's finding it hard to adjust to civilian life."

Finlay pulls a face as if he understands. "I see. I did wonder if there was something. He came across as a little... distracted, shall we say. As if he had a hell of a lot on his mind. Do you know where he's staying while he's here? That was something else my colleague should have taken down but didn't." He rolls his eyes.

I blow out a breath. "I think he was camping. But I'm not sure which campsite, sorry." I figure this is vague enough without being a lie.

"It's the weather for it, at least," Finlay says and smiles. At that moment I know I've swerved this particular bullet.

"It certainly is," I say, herding them out of the kitchen and along the hallway to the front door. "We're not used to all this sunshine, are we?"

"Well, don't knock it," Finlay says as my shoulders relax some more. "And thank you for your time, Mr Wilkes. If you do think of anything..."

"I'll give you a call!" I hold up the card I'm still holding.

The officers both smile and nod their goodbyes as I open the door for them. Once they've left, I close the door and am about to go back into the kitchen to make a cup of tea to further calm my nerves, when Jessie appears at the bottom of the stairs.

I'm feeling slightly giddy after what just happened, so I don't notice her expression right away, but when I do, her intense stare and angry mouth send a fresh surge of adrenaline shooting through my system.

"What the fuck is going on, Rob?" she says. "And don't you dare fob me off this time."

After Jessie juts her chin at me for the second time I know I have to say something. It feels as if we've been standing here forever and I've still not been able to form any words since she stormed downstairs.

"Nothing is going on," I tell her.

"Bullshit!" She barges past me into the front room.

"Jessie, wait." I follow her in there.

"Keep your voice down," she snarls. "I've just got Noah down to sleep."

You were the one who was shouting, I want to say. But I don't. This is no time for sarcastic comments or clever one-upmanship.

"Please, Jessie, can we both calm down?"

"Tell me what's going on. Now. Between you and Dan."

I hold my hands out to her. "Baby, I swear... There's nothing—"

"That's crap, Rob, and you know it. What did the police want? Why were they asking you about the body in the reservoir?"

I fold in my lips to moisten them. "I don't know... I mean – I do. Dan went to see them. He told them this stupid tale about how he had a vague memory of seeing something on the roadside one time when we were driving home. I don't know how he thinks he can remember this, but he said it was that same summer when the man died. But it was probably a sheep. The police think so too. Did you hear them say that part?"

She doesn't respond to this but instead folds her arms and sniffs. "Something's going on. I can read you like a book, Rob. Why are you lying to me? Please, tell me what's going on."

"Not this again," I growl. My jaw throbs with tension.

"You promised me," she says as once more her rage shifts to sorrow and her voice rises a few octaves. "That night in the hotel after Jonathan's wedding. You promised me. No more secrets. You know what I went through in my past relationships. You know how hard it was for me to trust you."

I go to her, but she shrugs me away. "Jessie. I'm not keeping anything from you. Not really." There's that dichotomy again. Because I really do believe what I'm saying to her. In my heart, I haven't any secrets. I've never cheated on her, never even thought about it since we got together. She knows *me*. The *real* me. I've shared more of myself with her than with anyone. But there are just some things I can't tell her.

For her own good.

And for mine.

Because if I'm honest with myself, my biggest fear if the truth comes out isn't prison, it's having her hate me.

Although, even as I'm thinking all this, another part of me knows – by keeping it from her when she knows something is wrong – all I'm doing is driving a wedge between us.

"It's Dan," I tell her. "I think he's mentally unwell. He's manic and saying and doing weird things. I'll be honest, I'm a bit worried about what he's going to do. He's down on his luck and not coping well with life and I think he's come back looking for me because he thinks I owe him. He hasn't said it outright yet, but I think he wants me to lend him money."

Jessie looks down. I hold my breath, praying this revelation might go some way in alleviating the situation.

"You're not going to give him any?" she asks.

I shake my head. I've none to give. But I don't tell her this. It's another secret, but one I'm only keeping to myself until she's emotionally stronger.

"I was going to go see him and tell him he needs to move on," I say. "I can't have him in my life."

"What's he got on you?" she asks.

I lick my lips. "Nothing."

She darts her head up at this and the tendons in her

neck ripple. She squints at me as if trying to work something out. "I don't believe you."

I almost do a double take. "I've just told you everything. For heaven's sake, Jessie. Do you know how much I'm having to deal with at the moment, what with Dan and the restaurant and...everything? I'm not sleeping. I'm working all hours God sends. If I'm not working, I'm worrying about Dan or you and the kids. I'm fucking exhausted."

It all pours out of me in one go. I didn't mean to say any of it, but I can't stop myself. When I'm done, I sense the atmosphere in the room has altered. Jessie looks at the carpet and makes a weird noise that's halfway between laughter and a whimper.

"Oh, poor little Rob. You're exhausted, are you? Really?" she looks up at me with tears in her eyes. "I cannot believe you just said that to me."

I open my mouth, realising now how it sounded. "I didn't mean that you weren't... Or that you—"

"I wish I was exhausted," she says. "But I'm so far beyond exhausted I can't even remember what it feels like. You swan around doing whatever you want while I'm here looking after that screaming baby all day and night. You're selfish, Rob."

"Come on, Jess." I take a step forward, but she retreats the same distance. "You don't mean that."

"I do," she says, fighting tears. "I hate you right now. I hate everything. You. Me. The kids. I hate my entire fucking life. You've trapped me here and I don't know what to do."

"Come on, Jess. We can sort this out. Together. Please. We just need to communicate with each other more. And lean on each other. We both need to. I'm sorry it's become like this. But it won't be forever, Jessica. I promise." I step forward again and grab her forearms as she tries to get away.

"Get off me!" she screeches, yanking her arms out of my hands. Instinctively I try to catch her, but she swipes me away and slaps me hard across the face. "Get away from me! I hate you! You're a liar!"

"I'm not bloody lying!" I yell back, unable to contain myself.

"Piss off."

She pushes me away and storms past me out of the front room and up the stairs. "Jessie," I cry after her. But she's not coming down. I pick a cushion up off the sofa and fling it on the carpet. It's a futile gesture and only makes me angrier at myself rather than giving me any sort of release.

My skin is burning hot and the muscles across my back and shoulders vibrate with pressure. I can't deal with this. Not now. Jessie feels trapped, does she? So do I.

So do I!

I gasp for air. It feels as if the world is collapsing in on me. I grab my jacket and car keys and head for the door. I don't tell Jessie where I'm going because I don't know. I just need to escape these walls and free myself from this pressure in my head before my brain explodes.

I've been driving for less than five minutes when a black cat runs into the road in front of my van. I have to slam my foot down on the breaks and, as I do, twenty years of repressed memories and unheeded guilt flood my system. I see the man's face in the moonlight, feel the pain in his body. We did that. We took his life. Snuffed it out. Then, rather than help him, we discarded his broken body as if he was an old coat or some other detritus – an irritation that needed getting rid of lest it ruins our lives.

But guess what?

Our actions that night have pretty much ruined our lives regardless. It's funny how the world works.

"Stupid fucking animal," I snarl at the cat as it slinks under a parked car.

My rapid pulse throbs in my neck and inner thigh. I grip the steering wheel tighter as if I'm holding onto the edge of a cliff. That's the way it feels.

And I'm shaking. My body is shaking. I look in the rear-view mirror and a blue Toyota is idling behind me. The road is too narrow for them to drive around me and I see the dark figure behind the wheel raise their hands as if to say, "What's going on?"

I hold up my hand so they can see I'm sorry and shift the stick into first gear. Inhaling and exhaling slowly and deeply to stave off another panic attack, I pull away and take the next left down Hall Meadow Road. My intention here is to pull over and get my head together but I find myself driving onwards, up Norfolk Street and down the side of the garden centre. Now I know where I'm heading. And where I need to go. The only place I'll feel safe. Maybe the only place I've ever felt safe.

I see the top of Dad's bald head through the window as I park up. He raises himself out of his chair and waves as I clamber out of the driver's seat.

I smile but don't wave. He's waiting for me at the front door as I get up to it.

"This is a nice surprise," he says cheerily, but then clocks my expression. "Is something wrong, lad?"

I nod. I don't dare speak in case I burst into tears there

and then on his doorstep. He steps to one side so I can enter, and I shuffle past him down the corridor into the front room. It smells like it always does, of pine air freshener and just the faint trace of cigarette smoke. This is despite the fact he gave up over fifteen years ago. It's a reassuring smell and it transports me back to a different time. To a time before that summer. I'm glad I've come here.

"Do you want a cuppa?" Dad asks, joining me in the front room.

I sit on the armchair facing his. Mum's old chair. "No. Thanks. Not yet." I gesture for him to sit, too, and he does.

"What's going on, Robert? *Is* something the matter?"

"Maybe." I laugh and lean forward, wringing my hands together over my knees. I meet his concerned gaze and I want to tell him everything. I shake my head. "How do you do it, Dad? How do you stay so strong and upbeat? I know life wasn't easy for you at times, but you were always there for me, and I knew I could always rely on you."

He sighs an awkward sort of sigh. "And people can rely on you."

"No. They can't. Not anymore. I've done bad things... I've messed everything up." I wipe at my eyes and Dad makes a compassionate tutting noise.

"Come on, now. It can't be so bad. You're a great dad and husband."

"I'm not. You were. I don't know how you did it."

He's quiet for a while and when I look at him, he's staring at the carpet, deep in thought.

"You know, me and your mother had our problems too, lad."

I sniff back. "Did you? I mean, I know when she got

sick and then... You know... I guess it was hard then. But before?"

"Oh, aye." He sighs again but this time it sounds resigned, full of remorse, even. "I don't know if I should tell you this. I always vowed to myself I wouldn't..."

I frown. "Tell me what?"

He makes a low growling noise. "I never told you any of this because I didn't want to upset you. And I wanted you to remember your mum how she should be remembered. She was a great lady and a wonderful wife and mother. She loved you with every inch of her being." He smiles. "But she had her problems. Like we all do. There were a few times in our marriage when she grew rather... unwell, shall we say."

I sit back as images and old memories flash across my mind. My mum was a kind and funny woman, very friendly to everyone she met and a real extrovert. But there were times when she didn't leave the house for days. And then...

"Did she go and live with her sister or something?" I ask as a hazy memory comes to me. "When I was about ten?"

Dad nods but doesn't look from the wall. "You were eight. And yes, that's what I told you had happened. But only because I wanted to protect you. As I say, I didn't want you to think badly of your mum. But there were a few months when she was shacked up in Todmorden with a man called Justin she'd met through a mutual friend. He was a right dickhead. He had a ponytail. She was ill and he didn't help her at all." He glances at me and when he continues his voice drops to almost a whisper. "Then she was found... standing on the Mottram viaduct."

I open my mouth. No. Not mum. But no words come out other than, "Shit."

Dad shrugs. "It was the only time she ever did anything like that. But it was an awful time."

"What happened?"

"A woman walking her dog discovered her up there, near the train station end. She was looking over the edge. She said she was going to jump, and no one could stop her. But she was a nurse, I think, this woman, and was used to talking to people in crisis. Luckily, after a while, she was able to talk your mum down. The police called me at work and took me down there. There were police vans and ambulances and all sorts. A lot of fuss we didn't need."

"Jesus, Dad!" I grab a tissue out of the box that Dad always has on the coffee table and dry my eyes. "I never knew."

"Good," Dad replies. "That's how I wanted it."

I give him the most reassuring smile I can muster under the circumstances. It appears the Wilkes men have a history of keeping secrets – of telling white lies. But I don't hate Dad for this. In fact, I love him more. Sometimes you need to keep things hidden to protect those you love. A silence descends between us, and something rises inside of me. It's not giddiness but it's not far off.

"I killed someone." My voice is so quiet I can hardly hear myself. It also doesn't sound like me. I say it again. "I killed someone, Dad."

I raise my head and so does he, so we're staring at each other. "What do you mean?" he says.

"The body that they found in the reservoir, who was dumped there twenty years ago. That was me. It was my fault. He was a homeless person, I think. Just minding his own business and we killed him. Me and Dan. We knocked him down in my car. Remember the sheep?" I look away. Tears run down my face, but I make no move to wipe them away. "I'm sorry, Dad. I'm so sorry."

He goes quiet again, but I don't look at him. Now I've ruined this as well. He'll never be able to see me the same way ever again.

Out of the corner of my eye, I see him rock forward and get to his feet. "Where are you going?" I gasp.

He walks over to me and places his hand gently on my shoulder. "To make some tea," he says. "I think we both could do with a cup. Then you can tell me everything."

17

I t takes me two mugs of tea and the best part of twenty minutes, but I manage to tell Dad everything. About how Dan and I drove over to Holmfirth for the folk night, how we met those girls and thought we were on a promise, then how we got too drunk to drive home but decided to do so anyway. He listens to all of it without comment, only bowing his head when I get to the crux of the horrendous tale. I'm scared to look at him, but I force myself to as I carefully explain how we hit a man and then dumped his body in the reservoir.

"We thought he was dead," I say. "I know that doesn't make it any better, but it all happened so fast. I can't even remember being one hundred percent conscious of my actions. I know that doesn't excuse anything either." I risk a glance in his direction.

He doesn't look up. "No," he says. "It doesn't."

"I'm so sorry, Dad. It was the worst thing I've ever done, and it's haunted me ever since."

Finally, he looks up at me, sporting the same expression of concern, bordering on confusion, that he's had since I started talking. But he doesn't seem angry. Not yet at least. There's plenty of time for that.

"When did this happen?" he asks.

"Late summer in 2002. August, I think. Near the first bank holiday."

He nods to himself. "Right, I see."

"Do you remember I told you I hit a sheep?" I stare into my palms. I can't believe I'm actually saying this out loud in front of him.

"That was the person you hit, was it?"

"Yes."

He sighs. "Jesus, lad. What a bloody mess."

I begin to cry. He's being kind and reasonable and I don't deserve him to be.

"I know it is," I sob. "I hate myself so much. And now the police are sniffing around and Dan's back in town leaning on me to confess to what we did. But I don't think that's what he really wants. He's just trying to screw with me, letting me know he could destroy me if he wanted to. He's sending me threatening notes and calling through with prank calls to the restaurant. I think he wants money to keep quiet. And I haven't got any, Dad. The restaurant is going better than it ever has done but I think it's too late. I've got so much debt and I'm scared I'm about to go under. In more ways than one."

"Hey, hey, hey. Come on, son." He gets up and sits on the chair arm beside me. As more tears roll down my face, he puts his arm around my shoulders. "Try and keep it together, hey? Getting worked up isn't going to help anything."

"I know but I can't help it," I whimper. "And maybe I shouldn't have help, anyway. I'm a bad person and I deserve to be in this shit. I should never... I should have..."

I suck in a deep breath to compose myself. "I wish I'd never gone out that night."

"Aye, but you did. And one thing life has taught me: there is no point in wishing things hadn't happened a certain way. Doing that keeps you stuck in the past forever. What happened has happened. It's what you do next that's important. It's all you've got control over."

I lean into him and he tightens his grip on me. For the first time in a while, I feel secure, and not like the ground is about to give way beneath my feet.

"Do you hate me?" I ask him.

"You're my boy," he says and his voice cracks. "I could never hate you, lad. I can't pretend I'm not alarmed or even disappointed that you didn't come to me with this at the time. What the hell were you thinking?"

"I don't know. I wasn't thinking!"

He blows out a long sigh and shakes his head.

He does hate me. I can tell.

I've lost him now, too.

I let out a terrible wailing sound, which makes me feel sick for so many different reasons. I'm so pathetic and weak.

"Rob! Come on. Stop that."

"I'm sorry. I've let you down."

"You did a terrible thing, son. Awful. I'm not going to pretend otherwise. And I suppose I'm still trying to get my head around it myself. But you've got a family of your own to think about now. It breaks my heart to think of Fern and Noah growing up without a dad."

I lean away from him. "What are you saying?"

"I don't know," he snaps and gets to his feet. "I don't know what I'm bloody saying. It's a lot to take in, is all this." He paces over to the bureau on the back wall and picks up a framed photo of Mum. I watch him as he gazes down at her. He's no doubt thinking he's glad she's not alive to see this. It would break her heart. Just like I'm breaking his.

"Dad?" I say.

He doesn't look up but lets out a bitter-sounding chuckle. "To be honest I always felt something had happened around that time. You seemed to change almost overnight. You went from a happy-go-lucky sort with the world at his feet to being distant and always up in your head. It was as if you had the weight of the world on your back. I thought it was due to your mum passing or you being a difficult age. I would never have imagined it was... this. I'm sorry I didn't pick up on it more."

"You've nothing to be sorry for, Dad."

He puts the frame down and returns to his armchair. "You do need to make a decision, Rob."

"I know. A part of me thinks I should go to the police and confess. A couple of officers came to see me after Dan went to see them. But again, I think he did that to scare me. I got the impression the police had no clue we were involved. One of them gave me his card. I think perhaps I should call him, tell him I want to make a statement or whatever it is you do in these situations."

Dad makes a low growling sound. He does it sometimes when he's thinking hard about something. "And will that make things right, do you think?"

"I don't know. Will I go to prison?" I look up at him, but he won't meet my eye.

"You ran somebody over, then got rid of the body rather than own up. The fact that you were drunk in charge of a vehicle and felt compelled to do what you did points to a certain amount of accountability and premeditation on your part. It'll be manslaughter, at best. But if, as you say, the fella actually drowned after you chucked him in the water – then who knows? I don't think they'll be very lenient."

"Right. Yes. Shit. I wish I knew what to—"

"Ah, for Christ's sake, Rob. Pull yourself together now! This isn't just about you! You've got a wife and two kids at home. They need you to be strong. Now I'll support you in whatever you decide. Okay? I mean it. I'm angry as hell at you but you're my son and I love you and that's the way it is. A long time ago I made a promise to myself that I'd always protect you and I'm not going to break that promise, even for this." I nod and am about to say something when he holds his hand up to stop me. "You killed a man, Rob. That's not something anyone can forget easily and you're the one who has to live the rest of your life knowing that. The question is, can you? You seem to have done all right in the past, but I can see now it's tearing you apart."

I sniff back a tide of emotion. "I was really good at disassociating from it, I think. And distracting myself with other things. When I moved down to London I recreated myself as a different person so that I didn't have to be connected to that memory. Does that make sense?" He shakes his head as if to say 'not really' and I know how he feels. As time goes on it makes less sense to me as well.

"If I don't... If I continue to keep it to myself... What do I do about Dan?"

"That is a tricky one. If he is blackmailing you, there's not much you can do about it without getting the police involved. How much do you think he wants?"

"He hasn't said. He hasn't actually said outright that's his plan. But I suspect it is. It makes sense..."

"Ah, he was such a good lad, as well. The both of you

were. Like brothers. It's a damn shame it's all come to this." He looks away and I can see he's got tears in his eyes. He rubs at his nose and then swiftly wipes them away with the heel of his thumb. "I wish I could help you out, Rob. I do. But everything I've got is tied up in the house and I did lend you that money for the restaurant."

"I know. I don't expect anything."

But I know what I have to do now. I puff out my chest and get to my feet.

Dad looks up at me. "What's going on?"

"I'm going to go see him," I say. "Dan. I need to find out what his game is once and for all. I can't live like this. Either way, I need to know my fate. Does he really want us to confess, or does he want me to buy his silence? Because I can't make a proper decision until I know which it is."

And whichever it is, I'll be strong and I will take full responsibility. This is my fault. All of it. Whatever happens next, I will deal with the consequences like a grown-up. It's the only way I'll ever be able to look my wife and children in the eyes. It's time for me to step up and take control of my life.

"Be careful, Rob," Dad shouts after me as I walk out of the room and down the hallway.

"I love you, Dad," I call back as I yank open the front door. And then I'm striding over to my car with more purpose and determination than I've felt in months.

18

I'm speeding along Cemetery Road on my way to the reservoirs when it hits me. I'm supposed to be at the restaurant this lunchtime.

"Bollocks!"

I screech the car to a stop and grab my phone up from the passenger seat. The display shows the time as 11:11 a.m. I remember Jessie saying once that this time of day had special significance. It's called an angel number or something, and if you notice it a lot it means the universe has got your back. Today I take that as a good sign, even if I don't believe in it the way Jessie does. Or did, at least.

Despite her business degree, she was really into numerology and other New Age stuff when I met her. It was strange to me that someone like her would be into such things, but I soon found these two seemingly opposing sides to her personality – the logical versus the spiritual – appealing. It made her seem enigmatic and gave her an elusive edge. Plus, if she'd only been business-minded or only into crystals, she might have been too much. As it was, she was perfect. To me, at least. She still is. She still can be.

As I turn the car around and drive to the restaurant, I make a promise to myself that when this is all over I'll sit down with her and have a proper chat. I'll tell her how much I love her and how much she means to me, and I'll sort out a proper structure for our days so I can take over some of the parenting responsibilities again. Hell, soon enough I'll have all day every day free if the restaurant goes under.

Pearl is the first person I bump into as I stumble through the back door into the kitchen.

"Whoa there, Chef. You're going to have an accident," she says as I bang into the counter on my way through.

"I know," I say, fighting for breath. "I'm in a bit of a rush, that's all. I've got a lot on today."

She flicks her eyebrows. "You're going to burn yourself out one of these days, mate. You need to do some meditation or something."

"Do you think it could help a lost cause like me?" I ask, scanning the room for any jobs that need doing. But everything looks to be in its place. Pearl must have arrived early and cleaned down ready for service. "Did you do all this?" I ask, waving my hand over the scene.

She grins. "Yep. All sorted. I'm trying for my promotion, aren't I?"

"Well, be careful. You might get it." I go through into the staff room. If I do all the prep and leave Pearl to run the service, I should be able to get up and see Dan early afternoon. I just want to get it over with.

"Have you seen the bookings for tonight?" she calls through, laughing as she does.

I walk back out. "No. Why? What do you mean?"

"Have a look." She gestures to the main space with her chin, and I go through and head behind the bar to where the computer linked to the online booking system is kept. Swiping open the touchscreen I click on today's date and scroll through the bookings. We're almost full but one entry catches my eye. Most of the names are written in lowercase or with one capital letter, as is the norm, but this one is in abrasive capitals. It's also not a real name.

CSJKNCVUKEWE.

I imagine the random letters were typed in haphazardly so the booking form would allow whoever it was to advance to the next input box on the form. It's the same story with the next boxes, which are supposed to be for collecting the email address and telephone number – just a series of random letters and symbols. But in the box for 'Any Other Info' there is a coherent message.

THIS ENDS NOW!

I stare at the words, muttering them under my breath as a wave of fresh anger heats my blood. That bastard. Trying to mess with me is one thing, but coming at me in my restaurant, where all my staff can see, that's unacceptable. Because what's next? Jessie? The kids?

No.

I won't have it.

I won't let that wanker terrorise me any longer. I tap on the screen and delete the booking before marching back through into the kitchen.

"What the hell do you think that's all about?" Pearl asks, snickering to herself. She stops as soon as she sees my face. "What's wrong?"

"Everything. Nothing. Don't worry about it." I screw up my eyes and wave my finger at her. "Listen, I'm so sorry to do this but can you handle the lunch service for me?"

I open my eyes to see her nodding in agreement. "Sure. Yeah. I suppose—"

"Thanks, mate. I've got something important I need to do and it can't wait. I know the place is in good hands with you." I pat her on the shoulder and am already heading for the back door as she calls after me.

"I really do deserve a promotion after this, boss!"

She's joking but she's right. If I get through the next twenty-four hours I'll consider it. But right now, the only person I can focus on is Dan Chapman, and what I'm going to do when I see him.

I FIRE up the car and twist the stereo on. Guns N' Roses is still selected and the guitar riff intro of *Out Ta Get Me* snarls angrily through the speakers. The subject matter is a bit too close to home but Axel Rose's irate energy fires me up as I pull out of the car park and drive along the high street.

The police unit is still there as I pass Norfolk Square, but the lights are off and I can't see any movement through the windows. Taking a left, I drive up Norfolk Road. Despite being lunchtime, the road out of Glossop is quiet for once and I put my foot down, thundering along the winding roads and taking the corners like a madman. Once again I'm slightly ashamed that I'm driving so dangerously considering what happened, but the anger inside me won't allow me to slow down.

For the first time since I realised Dan could be a threat to me and my family, a thought hits me. At first, I shake it away, telling myself I'm being ridiculous and I shouldn't think such things. But the gloves are off and Dan has now shown his true colours.

So, could I do it?

Could I kill Dan to protect myself and my family?

I mean, obviously, if the crazy bastard was in my house with an axe threatening us physically, I wouldn't think twice about it. But this is very different.

As I drive on, my imagination goes haywire. As far as anyone else knows we're old friends. If it came down to it, anyone who knew the two of us back then would tell the police we were inseparable. I have no obvious motive to kill him. But who does...?

Bloody hell!

Didn't Dan mention something about having heat on him back in Brighton?

If there are bad people after him, it's not unfathomable they would catch up with him eventually and do him in. If he was found dead, that would be the logical conclusion to his demise. Unless you know the bigger picture. And as far as I know, only Dan and I are privy to the sickening truth of the matter. Well, and now Dad.

Bugger... Dad.

If Dan is murdered, then Dad will know straight away it was me who did it. He might be doing everything he can to accept and love me after what I told him earlier, but that would be too much even for him. I could see in his face before how hard he was finding everything I was saying. I'm his only son and he wants to protect me but he's not Don Corleone. He's an honest, gentle, law-abiding man. With strong principles. If he found out I'd killed Dan, that really would be the end of our relationship. I wouldn't blame him if he called the police himself and turned me in. Right after he washed his hands of me.

I can't have that.

I grip the steering wheel and shake my head to try to remove such a dangerous notion. But I could scare Dan off. I could make him believe I'm ready and capable of killing him if he doesn't leave me and my family alone. That way I'd only be playing him at his own game.

I'm mulling over how best to approach this when I get up to the lay-by close to where he's camped out and bring the car to a stop. A part of me wants to stay in the car a while longer, to work out some plan of action, but that would only be delaying the inevitable, and a stronger, angrier part of me has me jump out of the car. Before I can change my mind, I clamber over the roadside wall and up the hillside.

Normally it would take about fifteen minutes to reach the section where the terrain flattens out and Dan has set up camp, but today I cover the distance in less than ten. By the time I reach his makeshift campsite, I'm sweating and have to gulp back big mouthfuls of air as I pause to assess the situation. The remnants of a fire, along with two plastic bags of rubbish tied up and pinned to the ground by rocks sit in front of his tent, which is now sagging considerably in the middle section. As I move over to it I see the tent entrance is unzipped open and the front flaps sway in the breeze. Leaning down, I look inside. It's empty. Immediately I straighten up and spin around, half-imagining Dan to be sneaking up behind me. But no one is there.

"Come on, Rob. Keep it together," I mutter to myself as I lower myself down into a crouching position to peer deeper inside the tent. Dan's rucksack is still there and a pile of clothes, which he looks to be using as a pillow, is positioned at the mouth of his sleeping bag. Near the opening of the tent is a small cardboard box containing two tins of baked beans, a carton of orange juice, a loaf of bread and a half-drunk bottle of cheap Scotch. As I shift the box to one side, I see a scuffed and dog-eared note-book sticking out from underneath and, glancing back over my shoulder once more, I reach down and pull it out.

Staying low, rocking on my haunches, I flick through the tatty notebook. Mostly it's full of weird doodles and basic drawings of birds done in scratchy black pen. They're not exactly the sort of drawings someone might find in a movie to indicate the other person is a demonic psychopath, but they're not far off. I flick past a few more pages and then stop when I come to a page of writing. The letters are spidery and erratic, the same as on the envelopes but written in lowercase rather than capitals, so it's hard to tell if they match. It looks as if it was written by someone who was incredibly angry or incredibly drunk at the time. My guess is they were both those things. A lot of the words are hard to decipher but there are certain phrases I can pick out, and as I read down the page, I realise it's a confession.

We killed someone in the summer of 2002... I was driving. Rob Wilkes was the passenger... his car... Dumped the body in the water... Filled up with rocks... Drove away.

Towards the bottom of the page, the note becomes more meandering and the writing even harder to read. The last thing I can make out is the words *ruined my life* written over and over again with no spaces between them.

Ruinedmyliferuinedmyliferuinedmylife

"Rob? What are you doing?"

The voice over my shoulder startles me to the point I feel as if I might have a heart attack. With my entire body tingling with a surge of fight-or-flight hormones, I leap up and turn to see him striding towards me.

"Dan! I—"

"Are you going through my things?" he yells.

"No!" A grey fog descends on me and I worry I might pass out or throw up. "I was looking for you."

"You're reading my journal!" he says, walking up to me.

As he confronts me I roll my shoulders back and raise my chin. He stops a foot away and glares at me. His face is twisted into a cruel sneer and it's like he despises me. I force myself to remain still and hold his gaze, hoping the flurry of chaotic activity going on behind my eyes isn't apparent. I've never feared Dan. As an adult, I've never feared anyone. But now I do. Up here on the hillside, there's something wild and unsettling about my old friend.

"Give it to me," he says, holding out his hand. "That's my journal."

Despite the intensity of his presence and the fact my instinct is to give in to him, I hold my ground. As he reaches for the notebook, I move it behind my back.

"I'd say calling it a journal is somewhat of a stretch, to be honest, mate." My voice is croaky and shaky, so the shade I've thrown doesn't really land. I go on. "I read your little essay. Your confession. Are you going to send that to the police?"

He huffs out a laugh. "Don't know. Maybe. Would you have a problem with that?"

"I've got a problem with a lot of things, Dan. The phone calls, the notes, messing with my booking system... You going to the police and telling them just enough that I get a visit from a couple of DCIs. What the fuck do you want from me?"

"What are you talking about, Robby?"

"Oh, come off it. I know what you're doing. You're trying to freak me out. You're screwing with my head so I'll be more compliant when you finally tell me what you want from me."

"I want to cleanse my soul!" he yells. "I want freedom from the shit going on in *my* head." As he says this, he thumps his fist against the side of his face. It does nothing for my nerves.

"Please, Dan," I say, holding out my hand to him, trying a different approach. "Think about my family. My kids. I get it, okay, I understand. I want to be rid of the guilt and the trauma of what we did as well. But this isn't the way. We have to support each other. Please, stop tormenting me. Go back to Brighton. Please. Or wherever. You can't live up here much longer, anyway. The weather will turn soon enough. It always does."

"I can't go back to Brighton," he spits. "And I've no idea what you're talking about. Notes... Phone calls... What booking system?"

I shake my head, feeling my adrenaline levels subsiding. "Come on, mate. It's over. I'm not doing this."

"Give me back my journal."

"Why? So you can send this letter to the police? Or my wife? Or the local paper, maybe? Is this just more blackmail bullshit?"

"Give it here." He lunges for it and I step back. My heel hits against something that feels like a spongey rivet of coarse grass and I stumble over.

"Hey! Get off!"

I land on my arse and before I can get up, Dan pounces on me and knocks me back. The impact slams all the air out of my lungs, but I fight him with all I have left, holding the notebook out at arm's length as he straddles me and grabs for it.

"No!" I yell as he gets his fingers on it. I push his head away but a sharp pain spreads through my cheek into my skull and rattles my vision. As the world zooms back into focus I realise Dan has punched me and is about to swing for me again. I shift my head in time so the second blow only catches me on my ear. It stings like hell, but I swing my arm across my face to counter a third attempt and then strike out with my elbow. It connects with something sharp and hard, and I sense Dan's weight shift off me. As it does, I scramble away, kicking wildly as I do in case he retaliates. Once I'm far enough away I get to my feet and turn around. Dan is also standing, the journal gripped to his chest. His nose is bleeding and as he grins at me his teeth look pink.

"I don't want to fight you," I tell him. "I just want this to stop."

He laughs. "That's all I want, mate."

"Leave me and my family alone," I tell him. "I mean it,

Dan." At this, he lets out a sneery laugh. I've had enough of this. The man is clearly unhinged. The person he was – the friend I had – no longer exists. I turn and begin to walk away. I was foolish to think I could reason with him.

"Twenty grand," he calls after me.

I stop. A cool breeze tousles my hair. I don't turn around.

"Twenty grand and I walk away. You never hear from me again."

I lower my head. And there it is.

I knew it.

I bloody knew it!

"Dan, I don't have twenty grand," I say turning back to him. He's standing in front of his tent but is looking down into the valley rather than at me. "I mean it. There's no way—"

"I need money, mate. I owe people. Twenty thousand pounds. I don't think that's unreasonable. At all. Then you're free. We both are. The police have nothing; you know that – even with me dropping a few hints. There were no witnesses and nothing tied us to the scene. We'll be fine. Just as long as neither of us owns up."

I wait for him to look at me, but he never does. "I don't have that sort of money. Every penny I have is tied up in the restaurant and times have been hard with the pandemic and all the other shit going on in the world. I think I'm going to have to declare myself bankrupt soon enough. So, no, it's not unreasonable. But it's also impossible." I wait another few seconds before walking away.

"I'm dead, then, mate," he calls after me. "Is that what you want?"

I don't answer. I don't stop walking.

"I'm going to have to go to the police, then," he continues, his voice breaking into a hoarse growl as he shouts after me. "You leave me no choice. It's the only way I can stay alive. I'll confess. Drop us both in it. We'll go to prison. That's what's going to happen, Robby."

"You do what you have to do, mate," I whisper to myself, and as I make my way down to my van it dawns on me that I mean it. If the truth comes out, so be it. I can't deal with the lies and the secrets and the not knowing my own fate any longer.

And maybe it's better this way. It's only what I deserve. But more than that, I have no more energy left to fight.

So, do your worst, old pal of mine.

I'm done.

AS I GET FURTHER down the hillside and see my van parked in the lay-by below, I have a strong urge not to return to it. I don't want to go back to work, or home, or to my Dad's or anywhere else. Not yet at least. I have an intense throbbing in both temples and I need to stay out in the fresh air. I need space.

I reach the corner of one of the dry-stone walls that snake around the hillside, but rather than climb the stile that will take me down to the roadside I clamber over the wall and head laterally across the next field and then the next one also. I don't know where I'm going, or what I'm going to do when I get there. I only know I have to keep walking for a while. I press on through the long grass before it turns to bracken and moss and the vast unforgiving moorland spreads out to the horizon.

I stop and sit on a large boulder sticking out of the ground. A hundred feet below me is the field where Dan and I used to go sledging. Where he broke his arm one year trying to 'snow surf'. We'd come here every year when it snowed, up until we were fourteen or fifteen when some kids from another school area got into serious difficulties and a young boy died. The mountain rescue teams had to be called out and I remember it was on the front page of the local paper. After that, our parents put a stop to us coming up here.

I lift my feet onto the boulder so I'm sitting with my legs bent and my arms wrapped around my shins. I can feel the cold rock through my jeans, but it doesn't bother me. Sledging here as a child seems such a long time ago. I remember I was such a happy kid, but I suppose I was lucky, too. I had loving parents and good friends. I did well enough at school that I could have done anything I wanted with my life if I'd put my mind to it. The whole world was in front of me. Right until that night.

Down below, I can see the reservoir and the spot where we hit the old man. It's sad that, even now with his remains being discovered, there's little anyone knows about him. Who was he? Where was he going? Normally the police can identify a John Doe from their dental records, so the fact they haven't done, and he didn't have any, points to the fact he was indeed homeless. Which, I suppose, could be seen as a blessing and a curse for the two kids who disposed of him so cruelly and thoughtlessly but who doomed themselves in the process.

I close my eyes and feel the breeze on my face. It's nice. For the first time in a long time, I feel free and light. I wish I was a bird so I could take off and fly away somewhere forever.

I open my eyes again and I'm still Rob Wilkes. I'm sitting on the hillside. What did I expect? Birds can't fly when they're so weighed down.

And yes, I made a decent run of my life regardless of what happened that summer. But I think deep down I always knew I was doing just that – running – and that one day my past would come back to haunt me. Every aspect of my world is crumbling to dust. My marriage, my livelihood, even my sanity. Is this what they mean by karma? Did it all start going wrong that night?

I screw up my eyes along with my fists and release a scream that has been stuck in my chest for days, maybe even years. It feels good and I let rip, screaming until there's not one molecule of oxygen left in my lungs. When I'm done, I feel lighter in my body, and I know what I have to do.

Something I should have done a long time ago.

Before I talk myself out of it, I pull out my phone, scroll to 'favourites' and call Jessie. I suspect she'll either be feeding Noah, or taking a well-deserved nap whilst he sleeps, and when it goes to her answering machine after three rings, a pyrrhic sense of relief ripples through me. But it also doesn't stop me. When the beep goes, signalling I should leave a message, I take a deep breath and go for it.

"Jessie, it's me," I say. "I'm sorry to do this on your answering machine but I don't think I could say what I need to say while you were in front of me or even able to respond. I just want to say my piece and have you hear it." I swallow but my throat is so dry it's difficult. "Okay, here goes. Firstly, I'm so sorry for being such a shit husband recently. I know you're struggling and I should be there for you more and take some pressure off you. But the truth is I'm up to my eyeballs in pressure myself. Fire and Ice is doing well but I think the last few years have done too much damage. I'm terrified we're going to lose the business." Tears and snot are pouring down my face but I don't stop to wipe them away. "That's not the worst of it, Jess. I know you think I've been keeping things from you and you hate me for it – with good reason – but I've not been able to tell you up to now because I'm terrified of what you'll think of me. It's bad, Jessie. Really bad. So bad I don't want to say it over the phone, but I will tell you. All I will say is it's got nothing to do with you or with us – it all happened before I met you. I did a bad thing a very long time ago. And the thing is, Dan knows and now he wants me to pay him twenty grand or he'll tell the police what I did. What he and I did. Oh shit, baby, I hope I'm making sense. I'm so fucking sorry."

I take the phone from my ear and let out a long whimper that immediately disgusts me with how pathetic it makes me sound.

Come on, mate.

Remember what Dad said. She needs you to be strong.

I take a second to compose myself and return to the call.

"I should have told you, straight away," I say. "I'm sorry that I didn't. I just wanted to protect you and the kids from it. But I know all I've done is upset you and made everything worse. Not that it could get much worse." I wince as I realise what I'm about to tell her. "I'm going to have to give Dan the money, Jessie. I don't have it to give, but I can get a loan, maybe. I'll have to sell the restaurant, but I don't know what else to do. All I wanted was to be a good husband and father and provide for my family. You're amazing and you don't deserve any of—Shit!" A shrill beep announces the end of my time and a woman's voice, mocking to my ears, tells me if I want to rerecord my message to hit '3'. I think about it. But what's done is done. And in so many ways.

I hang up and am alone once more. It's just me and the barren, unforgiving landscape. Just me and the sky and the A6024 down below. The road where I killed a man. The road where my life changed forever.

19

I'm not sure how long I sit up on the hillside but by the time I get back to the van the time on the dashboard clock says it's almost two. Lunch service will be all but over by now and I consider driving back to the restaurant and helping Pearl and the rest of them with the clean-down. I don't want to face Jessie until I know she's listened to the message, and a bit of grunt work will take the focus off my problems for a short while.

Busy hands, quiet mind...

I set off driving but as I park the van in the car park around the back of Fire and Ice and glance in the rear-view mirror it dawns on me that I can't face my staff right now. Not only do I have dirty tear marks running down my face, but if any of them smiled at me or showed even the remotest semblance of concern, I think I'd crumble. I consider driving over to Dad's place and I imagine him seeing my car as I pull up and waving at me through the window like he often does. I so want to see him right now. I want him to beckon me inside with a smile and wave. I want him to make everything okay again.

I close my eyes and lean back against the seat. It feels as if I've not slept properly in weeks and a benign blanket of numbness descends on me. I long for oblivion, to not be me for a while. Maybe forever. I let out a long sigh and I can feel my system relax. I know in that moment that I won't have this hanging over me for much longer. It's not exactly a nice feeling but there is some relief to be found in the knowledge. This is what rock bottom feels like.

I hunker down in the warmth of my coat and drift further into the silent void of sleep. Once there, I see the old man again, but this time he's not racing towards me through the darkness but standing, peacefully, at the side of the road. I drift over and he smiles as I stand in front of him. I bow my head as I speak with him.

I didn't know what I was doing.

I was young. I was foolish.

And I'm sorry.

I'm so very, very sorry.

I yearn for him to respond but he doesn't. When I look up his face has changed. It's now Dan looking at me. His eyes widen with insanity and greed.

No. Go away.

I don't want you here.

This was going so well.

It was all going so well...

"Rob! Chef!"

A dull banging in my head breaks the spell. I open my eyes to find myself sitting in a car. My car. Or, rather, the work van. Jessie has the car today. More banging. I look to my right to see Simone standing next to the door. She smiles and waves as I notice her. I shuffle around wondering how best to open the window with the engine off but then she opens the door herself.

"Sorry to wake you," she says, peering around the gap. "I wasn't sure what to do. But I didn't think you'd want everyone to see you here on their way out."

"No. Thanks." I rub at my face. "What time is it?"

"Three-ish, I think. The lunch service is over."

Shit.

I grab my phone from the passenger seat. The time on the screen says 3:07 p.m. Jessie must have listened to her answering machine message by now, but there are no missed calls from her. There are no messages at all. That's weird.

Weird and worrying.

I open up Facebook to see if she's posted anything recently but before it opens my phone beeps to tell me the battery is about to die. I get to scroll through my feed for a few seconds but see nothing from her before the screen flashes and goes black.

Bloody hell.

I can't get a break at all right now.

I fling the phone onto the seat beside me.

"Service went well," Simone says, as I yank the seat belt over me. "It was busy, too."

"Great. Thank you so much for handling it," I tell her, rubbing at my face some more. "And I'm sorry you found me like this, Simone. I'm just a little worn out, what with the new baby and everything."

She frowns. "Of course. It's just... Are you sure you're well, Rob? Maybe you should take a few days off? We can handle—"

"No!" I snap. "I'm fine. I mean... Maybe I will. I don't know. Sorry, I can't think about it now. I have to go."

I grab the door handle and ease it closed so she has time to let go. Through the window, I see she still has a concerned expression on her face, so I wave and smile before starting the engine and pulling out of the car park.

I need to get home.

I need to see Jessie.

Every traffic light is on red as I drive back along the high street and I wonder briefly if this too is the universe fucking with me. I remember Jessie saying once how everything we experience in the world is a projection of our own internal thought process – or something like that. I dismissed it as utter crap at the time – though obviously not to her – but maybe she had a point. It sure feels as if my negative emotions are seeping through my pores and poisoning the world around me.

I pull into our drive ten minutes later and after retrieving my phone I'm out of the van and running across the gravel drive towards the front door. I notice that the car isn't here but it's almost 3:30 p.m. and Jessie will be picking Fern up from pre-school. She'll be back any minute and I want to be ready for her. I unlock the front door and go inside.

I stride through into the kitchen. Cups and dirty plates litter the table and a curled crust of bread lies on the tiled floor in front of the bin.

The lounge isn't much tidier. There are cushions on the floor, more dirty cups and one of Jessie's nursing bras laid out across the coffee table.

I lift my phone to check the time and remember the battery is dead. Going back into the kitchen, I plug it into the charger we keep next to the toaster and head upstairs.

The house feels empty and devoid of life at this time of day. There's a heaviness in the air that's almost stifling. I put my head around the door of Fern's room, seeing the usual explosion of Barbies, Lego bricks and stuffed animals. I tidy everything up most nights, as best I can, but she only needs a few seconds each morning to ruin all my hard work.

Once done I walk the short distance across the landing to our bedroom. The lights are off and the curtains are drawn. I stride over and slide them open to let light in. The room is a real mess. The bed hasn't been made and clothes and underwear are strewn over the floor and piled high on the chair.

What is going on?

I'm about to leave the room when something on the floor catches my eye. I turn on the light and walk down to the end of the bed. Fern's box of craft stuff is sticking out from underneath it.

What the hell is that doing in here?

I pick it up, about to walk into Fern's room when I look down and see what's inside. When I do I stop dead and wilt into a sitting position on the edge of the bed as my legs lose their grip on the world.

"What the hell...?" I whisper to myself. "No, Jessie. What have you done?"

Lying on top of the box is a piece of white paper and stuck on the front of it, in a selection of large cut-up letters, are the words:

STOP! NOW!

I rifle through the box. Along with Fern's brightly coloured feathers and pots of glitter and glue, there is a stack of old magazines and newspapers. As I lift the first few out, I see most of the pages have been hacked up with scissors and most of the letters cut out from the headlines.

Shaking my head, I lift out the magazines and find

some more notes at the bottom of the box. Rejects, perhaps. I flick through them.

TELL THE TRUTH

I KNOW YOU LIE

NO MORE SECRETS

I don't think I've taken a breath since I found the box and I feel lightheaded. I place the box beside me on the bed and suck in a deep breath, holding it in my lungs in the hope it will help slow my heart rate or stop the nausea from rising within me.

Jessie did it.

Jessie sent the notes.

But, why? I don't understand.

Did she know about what we did? Has she been stringing me along all this time?

With a fresh burst of dark thoughts spinning around in my head, I get up and go downstairs. My imagination is now on overdrive as I stagger through into the kitchen. I'm even considering the possibility that Jessie somehow knew the man we killed – and has been playing some elaborate, fucked-up long game for all the time we've been married.

But no. That's stupid.

She loves me.

I know she does.

My mouth is dry, and I go to the sink to get myself a glass of water but on the way over there my recently charged phone begins to ring.

As I go over to it, I see my Dad's name on the caller ID. I grab it up and swipe it open.

"Hey," I say. "It's me."

"Robert! Thank heavens. I've been trying to call you for the past forty minutes." He sounds frantic. He sounds like I feel. "Where have you been?"

"Sorry. My phone died. What's going on?"

"You need to come over here, son. Now."

I glance around me; the room starts to spin. "Why? What's going on?"

"Please, Rob. We'll talk when you get here," he says. "But it's Jessie, Rob. I'm worried about her. And you should be too."

20

I bring the van to a screeching stop outside my dad's house a short time later. I've no idea how long it took me to get here. In fact, I've not much recollection of the journey at all, having driven on autopilot for the entire time, whilst I struggled to stay out of the murky recesses of my imagination.

Dad is standing in the window as I get out of the van and he opens the front door as I race down the path.

"What's going on?" I ask him.

He glances over my shoulder and grabs hold of my arm. "Inside, come on."

I walk past him and into the front room where I see Fern lying on the rug colouring in a picture of a unicorn. She looks up at me and grins. "Hi, Daddy. I'm doing you a picture."

"Brilliant, thanks, darling." Noah is in Dad's armchair, asleep in his carry seat. I spin around to face Dad as he follows on behind me. "Where's Jessie?"

"That's what I want to talk to you about. Let's go into

the kitchen." He raises his head and his voice as he addresses Fern. "You'll be okay for five minutes, Ferny, won't you? Just need to have a chat with your daddy in the other room. It's only boring grown-up stuff."

She doesn't look up from her colouring book. "See you soon," she says.

"Fern, darling," I add. "Can you do Daddy a massive favour and watch your brother for me like a big girl? If he wakes up, come and get me, okay? I know you're such a great big sister and you can do that, yes?"

"Yes, Daddy." She still doesn't look up.

Good enough.

I follow Dad through into the kitchen. "Where is she?" I ask again.

"The short answer is, I don't know. I'm so sorry, Robert. I tried to keep her here but there was no stopping her without physically restraining her and I didn't want to do that."

"No, of course not. But she's safe? You don't think she's going to do anything... stupid?"

Dad shakes his head in a confounded sort of way. "I bloody hope not."

"What happened?" I bring my hands to my face. They're shaking. "When was she here?"

"She arrived about an hour ago, banging on the front door whilst I was doing the washing-up like she was trying to break it down. She asked me if I'd watch the kids for a while. She said she had something very important she needed to take care of."

"Did you ask her what that was?"

"Aye, I did. But she wouldn't say." He places his hand on my forearm. "But it wasn't just that, Rob. There was something about her that really bothered me. Has she been okay recently – in herself, I mean? Have you noticed her acting odd?"

I shake my head. "I don't know. Yes. Maybe. I've been so busy with work and stuff that we've not had much time for each other. I know she's been struggling a bit since Noah was born, and I've found her just sort of staring at the wall or out of the window a few times but..." I grit my teeth.

Bloody hell!

I should have been there for her.

Has she left me? Has she had enough?

I've no idea what to think or believe. I can't get my thoughts in any sort of order.

"What are you saying?" I ask. "Is she a danger to herself? Or the kids? Or has she just legged it?"

"I can't answer that, son," he says. "It's just... the way she was staring at baby Noah before – it was like she thought he was some evil force. It worried me. It also reminded me of something."

"Of what?"

"Let's sit down," he says, pulling out a chair and gesturing for me to do the same. We sit and I lean over the table, clenching my hands together to stop them from shaking as he composes himself.

"Dad?"

He inhales deeply. "Okay, so... You know your mother struggled at times? With her mental health, I mean. Well, that look that Jessie had in her eyes before, I recognised it from when your mum was sick."

"When she tried to... jump off the viaduct?"

He looks down as a melancholic smile spreads across

his face. "Aye. But I think I implied before that she got better after that. But that's not the full story. Your mother struggled off and on with depression for quite a while. For most of her life, truth be told. I did my best to protect you from the worst of it. And before I go on, I want you to know she was a good mother and she loved you with all her heart. I made sure you knew that. And we had good times, didn't we?" I nod and he smiles again, and I want to cry. I beckon for him to continue. "It wasn't her fault, you see. When you were born, she had what they called then post-natal psychosis. I'm not sure what they call it now. She found it very difficult to cope, and of course, there wasn't the same sort of paternity leave as there is now. I think I had three days off with you, then I had to go back to work. I'd often come home to find you screaming and her just... staring at the wall."

I watch him, not wanting to look away for a second. "And you think...?"

"Possibly. Like I say, Jessie had that same look in her eyes that your mum would get. An intense but faraway expression. As if she was here but not here, and that she had too much going on behind her eyes for her to deal with. But the thing is you can get it sorted these days. We didn't have that same luxury back then. People didn't discuss mental health the same way they do now. They gave her various pills over the years, and some helped, some didn't. But she suffered from it right until the end. It was one reason why we didn't have any more children after you. But you were enough, Robert. You were more than enough for both of us."

It feels as if my heart is going to explode. I open my mouth but no words come to me, so I close it again. I want to scream and cry. I want to run out of the house and find my wife. I need to tell her I'm sorry and that I'm going to help her. I'll do whatever I need to from now on, whatever it takes.

But it all makes sense now.

Why the hell didn't I see what was going on right in front of me?

And did I cause this? Did she know somehow I was connected to the body in the reservoir? Is this what has tipped her over the edge? She's no fool. She'll have put two and two together. I should have told her as soon as they found the body. She'd have understood. Maybe...

Idiot!

You bloody idiot!

Dad must sense the pain and confusion overwhelming me because he reaches over and rests his hands over mine. His palms are still rough and calloused despite him being retired for the past five years.

"And you think Jessie has the same condition Mum had," I whisper. "Post-natal...?"

"Psychosis. Aye. I do. She came in here like a whirling dervish, asked me to watch the kids and was saying all sorts of weird things about you and her. I tried to talk to her, to get her to slow down, but she was off before I could stop her. I've been ringing you ever since."

"Oh, Dad," I whisper. "What am I going to do?"

STOP! NOW!

An image of the note I found in our room flashes in my mind and a fresh thought hits me. If it was Jessie who sent the notes, it's also likely she was the one calling the restaurant and sending threatening messages via the online booking system. Her reasoning behind these actions is obviously incredibly troubling but it means one thing. Dan wasn't behind any of it. His aim might have always been to try and get money out of me, but he wasn't being creepy about it, he wasn't fucking with my head the way I thought he was. That still doesn't help me understand why my wife was doing this, however.

"I need to get Jessie some help," I say.

"Aye. And you will. Your mum never got the support or the help she needed but as I say, it was different times. There are lots of things that can be done these days."

"I need to find her first," I say, rising from the table.

"There's something else, Rob," Dad says, holding his hand out. "Something Jessie said."

My heart does a somersault. "What was it?"

"It's nothing, I suspect, just her mind playing tricks on her. But she said you'd been cheating on her. That your old friend was back in town and that he was evil and was making you evil as well. I told her I didn't believe that was the case, but she wouldn't have any of it. She said you were back to your old ways, keeping secrets, telling lies, doing things behind her back. But don't worry, son, it's just part of the illness. When she's better again she'll know that you would never—"

"Bloody hell, Dad," I gasp, as a bad feeling blossoms in my stomach.

Secrets. Lies. The notes. It was never about the body. She thinks I'm cheating on her. She thinks Dan is involved and is leading me astray. And in her current state of mind...

"I've got to go," I call back as I head for the front door.

"Rob? What is it?" Dad hurries after me.

I get to the front door. "I don't want to say, not yet." I face him. "Can you watch the kids for a while longer?"

"Sure. But where are you going?"

"I think I know where Jessie is," I tell him. "And I need to find her before something terrible happens."

21

The first set of traffic lights I come to are on red.
Typical.

"Come on! Please!" I yell at them, slamming
my palms on the steering wheel. "I don't need this today."

How can I have been so blind to my poor wife's needs?
I knew something was wrong but I had no idea she was in
such a dangerous state of mind. I hate myself and I hate
that I've been so focused on my own shit I've not been
able to look after my family properly. What sort of
husband am I? What sort of father? I should have seen
this coming. We could have got her support and help
weeks ago. She could be on her way to recovery right now
if I hadn't had my head stuck up my arse. The kids seem
fine, but who knows what Fern has seen or heard since
her mum fell ill? It's not Jessie's fault. It's mine. I'm the one
who should have shielded his daughter from her
mummy's illness. I should have protected her from the
stark realities of life. Like my dad did for me.

The light turns green, and I speed away, driving down

Bank Street and through the centre of Hadfield. I pass the train station and Dan's mum and dad's old house before joining Cemetery Road and taking a right onto Woodhead Road. Here I shift into fifth gear and put my foot down. I'm not far away now but every second counts.

"Please be okay," I mutter to myself. "Please don't do anything stupid."

I'm not sure if I'm talking to Jessie, myself, or Dan. I just want to make everything all right. And I will do.

Given half the chance, I will do.

As I drive on, memories of other instances come to me. Things Jessie has said and done over the last few weeks that in hindsight now seem strange. She wouldn't let me touch Noah for the first few days, then she complained I was ignoring him and that I didn't love him or her. I dismissed it then as her being exhausted and I suppose it was another stressful situation I didn't want to deal with. Now the veil of my own selfish paranoia has been whipped away I see the stark truth of the matter. She is ill and she has been for weeks and weeks. But good old Rob Wilkes – Husband and Father of the Year – was too caught up stressing about his restaurant and then the body in the reservoir to consider there might be more pressing issues closer to home that required his attention.

Self-centred prick.

But no more. I make a quick deal with the universe that if it keeps Jessie safe, I'll be the best husband and father I can possibly be. I'll focus on my family above all else and do whatever I can to protect my kids and make my wife happy.

As I drive around the bend overlooking the first reservoir, I see our car parked in the lay-by a hundred metres down the road. I was correct. I wish I wasn't, but there we go, my life is full of pyrrhic victories presently. I bring the van to a stop and jump out, not stopping to even lock the doors as I jump the wall and race up the hillside. As I trek, I once again pray to the universe, or God, or whoever or whatever might be up there listening, that everything will work out okay.

Please let me find her.

Please don't let me be too late.

Don't let her or Dan have done anything stupid.

Stupid. What a ridiculous euphemism we use for such terrible things. A pathetic catch-all term when we fear someone has committed the worst possible act. I shake the thought away as I press on. I don't want to think about what might have happened. Not for the first time recently, I instruct myself to focus only on the present, on things I do have control over.

My heart does another somersault as I reach the point on the hillside where it levels off. Dan's campsite is a few hundred metres away from here, but my wife's sitting on a patch of bare earth a few feet away.

"Jessie," I gasp. "Thank God."

I stand and watch her for a moment, expecting her to say something or at least acknowledge me. But even though she's looking my way, she doesn't make eye contact. In fact, her expression doesn't change at all and she stares right through me. Her eyes are bloodshot and puffy and her skin and lips are the palest I've ever seen them. Her wavy, strawberry-blonde hair wafts in the breeze but there's a strand in her mouth that she makes no effort to remove.

"Jessica," I whisper, taking a step closer. "It's me, Rob."

She doesn't answer. She looks catatonic.

"What are you doing up here?" I try.

Nothing.

"Have you seen Dan?" I say. "He's been camping up here. You can see his tent over there if you look."

I point but she doesn't turn her head. She scowls and sticks out her bottom lip, the way Fern does when she's showing you that she's thinking. "Dan? Yeah. I've seen him."

"Oh? Right." I shuffle another half-step towards her. I don't want to freak her out. "Where is he? Is he in his tent?"

"I don't know." She returns to staring across the valley. I adjust my position so I can see her face. Her expression is chilling in its neutrality. I raise myself on my toes to peer across the terrain at Dan's campsite. There's no sign of him, but it looks the way it did the last time I was up here.

"Did you speak with Dan, Jessie?" I ask.

She nods slowly and her mouth twitches into a smile, but when she speaks, I detect a bitter tone in her voice. "Oh yes. I spoke with him."

"Okay. Good. And did he say where he was—"

"I told him I knew what he was up to," she snaps, suddenly animated. She glares and points her finger at me like she's trying to spear it through my heart. "I told him he was an evil presence and that he had to leave us alone. You see, I always knew you were a cheat and a liar, Rob. But you're weak-minded, too. You let the badness in too easily. You promised me over and over, but I knew it. Secrets are horrible things. They eat away at you. I hate them."

"I know you do." I hold my hand out. "Me too. But I've never cheated on you, Jessie. And I never will. I love you. You and the kids are my entire world." I've no idea if this is the right thing to say to someone in her state of mind, but I'm desperate and grasping at straws. "I know I've been distant recently, and I hate myself for being like that, and I'm sorry – but it's only because I'm worried about our finances and didn't want to worry you with all that. Not so soon after Noah was born and—"

"God help us!" she yells and tilts her head back as if she's about to howl into the sky. "I never thought it would be with a man."

What?

I lean forward, holding out both hands now. "What?"

"I listened to your message," she says. "Sure, you sounded all sorry and apologetic, telling me how Dan's threatening you and wants money from us. But I could read between the lines. I knew what you really meant. I just can't believe I fell for your lies for so long." She laughs and it might be the most chilling laugh I've ever heard.

"You've got this all wrong, darling. I swear to you. Dan is an old friend, that's all. And I see now he's not even a friend. You're right, he is bad news and I've told him not to bother us anymore. I'll get rid of him. I swear to you. Please. Let's just—"

"You and that man have brought evil into my life," she hisses. "And do you know what, Rob? I thought you were different. I thought you were one of the good ones. But more fool me, hey? Was this your plan all along? Fill me up with screaming babies and make me look after them so you can run about and have fun with whoever you want? Well, it stops now, Rob. I won't do it. I won't have it."

"Darling, please. I know I've been unfair recently, but I've had a lot on my mind and from now on all I'm going to do is look after you." I move closer, hands raised in case I spook her. But it doesn't look as if anything could infiltrate her resolve. There's a chilling acceptance in the way she's sitting and in the tone of her voice. I don't like it. "I'm going to help you if you let me. Shall we go, Jessie? It's getting cold up here. Why don't we go home, and we can talk there."

"I never thought it would be a man," she mutters. "But there you go. You think you know someone. And now he wants to take my money, too. I bet you put him up to it, didn't you? But don't worry. It's all over now. I made sure of it. He won't come between us anymore."

I'm about to say something else when I stop.

"Oh, Jess. No. What have you done?" I glance over at the campsite. There's no change. No sign of Dan. "Where is he, Jess? Where's Dan?"

She looks at me with empty eyes. "Sorry, Rob. I'm afraid your evil plans are over."

I stumble past her, driven on by a mixture of grim curiosity and dread.

Please, no. She can't have...

She wouldn't have...

I quicken my pace until I get to Dan's campsite, and as I walk around the front of his tent it feels as if my heart and lungs have dropped into my stomach. I slump to my knees, holding my hands up to my mouth as I peer through the opening of the tent. Dan is there, lying inside his sleeping back. He looks to be asleep. In fact, I might think he was if it wasn't for the rock as big as my fist that's lying on the groundsheet next to his head. Fresh blood, still wet, runs down one side of it.

"Oh, God, no," I whimper to myself as I shuffle forward to get a better look. Dan is facing away from me but as I put my head inside the tent, I see the blood covering his face and the sickening dent in his forehead where the rock crushed his skull.

I swallow back a mouthful of bile.

Where *Jessie* crushed his skull.

Dan is dead.

My wife has killed him.

22

I don't know what to do! It feels as if the world is closing in on me and I can't breathe. I back out of the tent and bend over the side of a large boulder to be sick. I retch and gasp but nothing comes up except for a small amount of foul-tasting yellow liquid which I spit out into the grass. Wiping at my mouth, I lean back and look over to where Jessie remains sitting on the ground and staring at the sky as if nothing has happened. As if she hasn't just smashed Dan's head in with a heavy rock.

Poor bastard. He must have been asleep when it happened. I wonder if he knew. The first blow must have woken him up. But after that, he was probably too disorientated and injured to fight back. He'd have died in a quagmire of confusion and pain. The thought makes me want to throw up again, but I gulp back air and steady myself.

What do I do?

What the hell do I do now?

Dan was a thorn in my side, and I no longer recognised him as the man I used to call my best friend, but he didn't deserve that.

I walk back over to Jessie and sit next to her. She doesn't respond at first but then leans into me.

"It's all going to be fine," she says. "We've got rid of the badness now. It's gone. It's just you and me again. Maybe we can move away? Somewhere quiet. We always wanted to go travelling."

"What about...?" I stop myself.

What about the kids, was what I was about to say.

What about the restaurant?

What about the fact that you've been sending me threatening notes and have just caved Dan's head in?

But none of those conversations are for now. She's ill. She needs help. But before that, I need to make a decision for both of us. And fast. I look around. I see Dan's tent. I see the valley and the road snaking up to Holmfirth where twenty years ago he and I also killed someone. Then I see my wife, her pale expression one of happiness now as she looks back at me. In that moment I know that I have to protect her at all costs.

This isn't her fault. It's Dan's fault and it's my fault. I'm not under the illusion that my telling her the truth about my past – or the real reason why Dan was in town – would have stopped her from becoming unwell. But if I'd been more responsive and alert to her state of mind, I could have caught that she needed help sooner. We wouldn't be in this position. Noah's birth, the body in the reservoir, Dan's arrival, the restaurant – it all added up to the perfect storm. But it doesn't excuse what I did. Or what I didn't do.

"It's going to be fine," I say, placing my arm around Jessie and pulling her closer. "I'm going to be a better man. No more secrets. Not between me and you, at least. Not once we've worked out what the hell we're going to do about this."

I give her a squeeze and then release her so I can get to my feet.

"Where are you going?" she calls after me.

I wave her down as I walk back to the tent. "Stay there. It's fine. I'm only going to be gone for a few minutes. I have to get something." At Dan's campsite, I scan the area for any sign that Jessie or I were here. I can't see anything but that doesn't mean the police's Scene of Crime unit won't find something. I turn slowly around on the spot, searching for tell-tale footprints in the dirt, or any stray hairs or clothing fibres attached to the long grass. Satisfied I can't find anything, I face the tent and before I can overthink it, I clamber inside. The air is stale and close, and I try not to look directly at Dan's battered face as I cast my attention around the space. My eyes land on the rock. Can the police dust for fingerprints on such an item? And even if they could, do they have Jessie's on record? I don't think so but as I look closer, I can see there's a print of her finger in blood on one side of it. That's too much to go on in my opinion. It's too telling. I pick it up, more than aware of the crushing realisation that I have now sealed my fate in terms of what happens next.

It has to be a cover-up.

Another one.

But unlike twenty years ago, this is about my wife's mental health and my kids' happiness. I have to do anything I can to ensure that none of this comes back on Jessie. As I'm exiting the tent with the rock, I glance around for Dan's notebook and lift a few items to search for it. It's nowhere to be found but that's fine. He probably got rid of it. It was mainly scribbles and gibberish anyway.

Once back outside, I get to my feet and consider what the hell I'm going to do with the tell-tale rock. Not for the first time this week, I wish that the damned reservoir was full of water. But as I scan the panorama I see that over in Torside Reservoir, near the sailing club, the water is more expansive than in other areas and looks to be four or five feet deep in the centre. I can't imagine the local police are going to send divers down on the off chance of finding the murder weapon, and all being well, if they do and they find it, the evidence will have washed away. It's a risk, but it's a calculated one and I'm out of other options.

Feeling more in control than I have done in weeks, I walk back to my wife. The blue skies of the last few weeks have turned to grey clouds, and she looks cold. I hold my hand out to her.

"Come on, Jess, let's go home."

She takes my hand and I help her down the hillside. On the way down I plan out the narrative in my head and what we'll say to the police. The first thing I need to do when we get back to the house is call Jessie's doctor and get her some proper medical help, but Dan's body will inevitably be found sooner or later. When it does, I expect the fact that I'm his old friend will mean another visit from DCIs Finlay and Wetherby. When that happens, I need to have my story straight.

Dan was a loner, I tell myself. He had many problems, including PTSD after his time serving in Afghanistan, but he was paranoid and delusional, too. I'll tell the police how he mentioned he'd left Brighton because he owed money to some bad people. It's not a big leap to think they followed him up north and killed him. Or if not them, someone else he'd pissed off over the years looking for retribution. Dan strikes me as the sort of man who had a long list of people with grudges against him.

As we reach the roadside, I'm feeling slightly more confident about our chances of riding this out.

"Where are we going?" Jessie asks as I climb over the wall and turn back to help her over. "Home, darling. We're going home. We're going to get you some help and get you better. It's all going to be okay."

And at that moment, I actually believe it myself. But then...

"Ah, bugger."

The van and the car are both parked up in the lay-by. There's no way I can let Jessie drive either one of them. But, no matter. I'll walk back for the car later. It's a long trek but so be it. With my arm around Jessie, I guide her over to the van and help her into the passenger seat. As I close the door a wave of serenity washes over me, which I find rather surprising but not unpleasant.

As I drive back to our house, Jessie leans her head against the side window. Occasionally she mutters to herself, but I can't make out actual words. At the first set of lights, I reach over and pat her leg and tell her not to worry. I tell her it's all going to be okay and I'm going to take care of everything from now on. And I mean it. I'll be the husband and father I should have been all along.

It's all going to be okay...

It's all going to be okay...

Regardless of me being one of the only people Dan was still known to in the area, there's no reason why the police will suspect I killed him. We were friends, for heaven's sake. Best friends. And, yes, they might think it odd that he didn't come to our wedding or that we hadn't seen each other in twenty years, but surely that only points to me having less motive to kill him? They'll have even less reason to suspect Jessie. She didn't know Dan. She has no motive at all.

Even if, by some miracle of police ingenuity, Finlay and Wetherby did suspect Jessie was involved, I suspect she could make an excellent case for temporary insanity considering her condition. No reasonable jury would convict a sick mother of premeditated murder. Yet, there'd still be a riot of procedures to deal with and plenty of questions to answer. I don't want her to be put through that. She's not well enough to deal with it.

It's better this way. As long as we stick to our story, we'll be fine. It's one more secret but it's a shared secret. A secret that will bond the two of us rather than rip us apart.

It's starting to get dark as we drive down to the far edge of Torside Reservoir and, once I'm certain there's no one around, and that I'm far enough around the curve of the water to be concealed from view from the sailing club, I throw the bloodstained rock as far as I can into the deep section of water. It lands with a satisfying splash and I watch the concentric ripples for a few seconds before brushing myself down and walking back to the van. Jessie is still muttering to herself as I climb into the driver's seat, but her eyes are closed and by the way her chest rises and falls, she appears calm.

I take her to Dad's house and we put her to bed in his spare room before I test out part of my newly formed narrative on him. I can't bring myself to tell him about what Jessie did – and I don't think I ever will – so I don't mention Dan at all. His concern is for Jessie's wellbeing and, once I've explained he was right about her condition and that I found her sitting on our front step staring into space, he appreciates the gravity of the situation and doesn't ask too many questions.

He's happy to put up Jessie and the kids for the evening and says I can stay over too, once I've picked up Jessie's car, which I'm grateful to him for. It might sound daft, but I feel that being near him tonight will make me feel stronger and braver, even. He's a good man, my dad. From now on I'm going to be more like him.

Once I'm sure Jessie and the kids are settled with Dad, I walk back for the car, taking as many back roads and country lanes as possible. Just in case. It takes me the best part of an hour but the exercise and fresh air help me to think and by the time I reach the lay-by I've convinced myself I'm doing the right thing. Dan is dead and it was tragic what happened. But we can't change that. There's no reason why my kids' lives should be ruined because of it. They need their mother.

And I'm aware this is the same sort of reasoning that went through my head twenty years ago. But maybe I was right then, too. Maybe sometimes you have to keep secrets to protect yourself and those you love. Guilt is a terrible thing to live with, but it can be done. I'm proof of that.

Once I'm in the car I drive to the restaurant. The evening service has just begun, and I make a big show of being seen by everyone. I say hello to all the staff, chat with Pearl and Simone and help Lawrence plate up a smoked salmon starter he's having trouble with – I even go out into the dining room and greet some of the customers. All this so they can tell anyone who asks that Rob Wilkes was working at Fire and Ice this particular evening. But it's good to be back in the throng of a working kitchen again, and after half an hour I'm fired up and feeling more optimistic than I have done in a long time.

So, let's hear it once again for good old Rob Wilkes and his uncanny ability to disassociate from his problems.

Or maybe I'm just so selfish I only care about things that concern me?

Whatever. I don't care. I'm full of adrenaline but for once it's the good kind, the kind that spurs you on to do good things. Heroic things. And it's not selfish. I'm doing this for my family, for my wife and children.

Dan was a broken, troubled man. He had no life and, whilst I'm not saying he deserved to die – and I will grieve for him once I have time to properly consider the fact that he's gone – he could have caused more problems for me down the line.

And it's over.

It's done.

Except for me and Dad, no one else knows how or why that body came to be in the reservoir, and that's the way it's going to stay. But that poor man won't have died in vain. Nor will Dan. I'm going to use this experience to turn over a new leaf. I'm going to make a proper go of the restaurant, I'm going to be the best father and husband I can possibly be. My new life starts this second. I'm stepping up, determined to care for my family above all else.

That's what my dad did for me.

That's how I make this okay.

PEARL SHUDDERS and the spoon she's holding hovers over the piece of turbot on the plate.

"Go on," I tell her. "You can do it. One quick flourish and it's done."

This is Pearl's first service in charge of making the halibut in beurre blanc with baby leaks and champagne foam. Fire and Ice's signature dish. I watch as she administers the spoonful of foam over the dish and steps back with a grin.

"There we are. Done!"

I lean over the plate, doing that chef thing where you wave the aromas up to your nose. But it does actually work. "It smells great and it looks great," I tell her. "Are you happy with it?"

She nods. "Yes, Chef."

"Great then, let's do it." I tap the bell on the counter. "Service!"

Simone appears and I smile at her as she picks up the plate, before turning back to see Pearl's excited expression.

"Thank you," she says. "For believing in me. I won't let you down."

"I know you won't. You're an amazing chef. I'm very lucky to have you on my team."

It's two weeks since I found Jessie up on the hillside and this is my last day in the restaurant before I hand over the reins to Pearl for a while. We still haven't hired a sous chef, but the rest of the team will chip in where needed to allow her to run the pass as well as be in charge of a few of the dishes. It'll be tough work but she's more than capable, and I can pop in if she needs me.

Up to now, I've been dividing my time between looking after Fern and working at the restaurant, but it's become clear I need to be at home. For many reasons. With today being Monday, Fern's day off from pre-school, my dad has taken her to the zoo whilst I sort out the handover. He's been amazing, as usual. I don't know what

I'd ever do without him. I know now how much he shoul-
dered for me over the years, regarding Mum and her problems. He must have been going through hell, yet he never
showed it and was always there for me with a smile and a
hug. If I can be half the dad to my kids as he was to me,
then I reckon I won't be doing too bad at all.

Our finances are still troubling me but I'm focusing on
what works, and with a bit of luck and the wind behind us
we should get through this dip and come out stronger.
Once Jessie is feeling better and is back home again, we
might even have cause for a double celebration.

The doctors were great when I called and explained to
them the extent of her condition. They sent us to a special
clinic for assessment a few days later and she was diagnosed with postpartum psychosis – which means she's
susceptible to hallucinations, delusions and mania. I'm so
glad we've got to the bottom of it. But a part of me hates
myself for missing it for so long. Never again.

Thankfully Jessie hasn't remembered what happened
with her and Dan up on the hillside, and I hope it stays
that way. Right now, she's in the hospital with Noah, to
help build their relationship under supervision whilst
she's being treated. The doctors have prescribed her a
course of antipsychotics and lithium to stabilise her
moods and she seems to be doing better already. It
means we've had to move Noah onto formula but the
transition was smooth and he's thriving. The doctors
think it's allowed for better bonding between mother
and son as well, as Jessie gets more rest now. I visit her
every day and the light in her eyes has returned even
after a week. This afternoon she even smiled at me
when I walked into her room. The doctors are already
saying she might be able to come home soon and with

some talk therapy and CBT, she should make a full recovery.

"Three halibut and one steak for table six," Simone calls out, shoving the printed order receipt across the pass.

I raise my eyebrows at Pearl. "What do you think? Can you handle three?"

"Yeah, I've got this," she says.

"Then get to it, Chef!"

I leave her to it and walk through into my office. The desk is still a sea of invoices and bills, but I plan to come in one afternoon this week when Fern is at pre-school and create a better filing system. Tidy desk. Tidy mind.

How we do anything is how we do everything.

I switch on the computer and out of habit go to the BBC news site and the local news section. The report of human remains being found in the reservoir and the connecting stories are still on the first page but there have been no new developments. The temporary police unit has also gone from the town square, and it appears the investigation into a possible cold case has been shelved. It's a big weight off my shoulders. I'll always have the guilt in my heart to remind me of what I did, but I can deal with it.

Dan's body was discovered five days ago by a group of ramblers and the discovery made the local news but there was no hint of it being linked in any way to the body in the reservoir, and there was no mention of an incriminating diary. The police came to see me about it, but it wasn't DCI Finlay and DCI Wetherby, who I was told were now working on a new assignment. I told the new officers as much as I felt was needed – that I'd not seen Dan for many years but that he'd reappeared out of the blue and told me he was hiding out here after upsetting someone back in Brighton. Thankfully, it turns out this was true. He owed a known local gangster a lot of money and, whilst the police didn't have enough evidence to arrest the guy for Dan's murder, they seemed to have made their minds up that he was responsible. In a way, I suppose he was. If Dan hadn't come back here, things could be a lot different.

I'm aware that sounds like quite a stretch and absolves me from a lot of blame, but I don't see it that way. I'm a good person. I'm a good husband and father. And I'm a good son. Sometimes good people do bad things, but that doesn't make them bad people. It makes them human. And it's not what you did in your past that matters. It's how you deal with it and move forward. I chose to find happiness with a loving wife and family, and even though it's sad and tragic and I do feel awful about what happened, it's not my fault Dan didn't make that same choice. He's as much to blame as I am.

The other stressful part for me, following Dan's body being discovered, was when my dad brought it up a few days later. He knew all about Dan trying to blackmail me, and whilst he didn't ask me outright if I was involved in his death, I could tell he was thinking it. Thankfully I'd just been informed by the police about Dan's involvement with the Brighton underworld, so I was well-prepped for the encounter. I told Dad what the police had told me, that these gangsters had caught up with him and that was why Dan was after money. I think he believed me, but there was a moment after I'd finished speaking where he stared at me for a few seconds too long and it felt as if the walls were closing in on me again. But then he smiled and wandered off into the kitchen to make some tea. Sometimes even the best of us believes what we want to believe.

Back in the office, I check my phone. It's almost 2 p.m. I turn the computer off and grab my coat.

"Am I okay to get off, Chef?" I ask Pearl as I go through into the kitchen. She looks at me and I hold up an imaginary watch on my wrist. "Visiting time."

She lifts her head and smiles. "Seeing as it's you. Give her all our love, won't you?"

"Sure, I will. And thank you so much for everything. Do you want me to help with anything before I—"

"Just get going, you soppy bugger," she says with a grin. "I've got this. We've got this."

I give her a sharp salute and head out, stopping in the staff room to grab the bunch of roses and hydrangeas I bought this morning. I've taken Jessie flowers every day since she was admitted to the hospital and her room is beginning to look like Kew Gardens. The nurses are even joking they'll have to go out and buy more vases if she stays in much longer. But I like doing it and Jessie seems to enjoy getting them. It's the little things that mean so much. I must remember that going forward.

It's raining as I get in the car and set off for the hospital, and it becomes even heavier as I drive down the high street. It's been like this for the past week and the reservoirs are already filling up. Soon they'll be full again and any more secrets they hold will be lost once more.

It's funny, I used to think I was a different person before that fateful night. And now I feel as if I've changed again into someone else. It's almost as if everything that happened regarding the body being discovered and Dan's return was experienced by a different person. Or, at least, a part of me that no longer exists. That part of me died up on the hillside with Dan that day. But it was also the part of me that was stuck in the past, unsure how to move on and give itself fully to the present. I expect I'll still get stressed and anxious at times, but I know I can cope with those things, and in time I hope the pain and anguish I've experienced will forge me into a better and more rounded person. Happier, too. Less selfish.

I park in the hospital car park near the front entrance and take the flowers through into reception, past an old woman with blue hair who's huddled over in the entrance, protecting her cigarette from the rain. It always amuses me how many people you see smoking outside hospitals. There's probably a depressing metaphor in there somewhere. We humans – we don't like to help ourselves.

The woman behind the counter recognises me as I approach – I'm probably known to them all here as Flower Man or something similar – and smiles as I pass by on my way to Jessie's ward.

I've got a real spring in my step as I walk down the long corridor and don't even mind the harsh stench of industrial cleaning products. I push through the double doors at the far end with just as much zeal. I'm excited to tell Jessie about Pearl taking over from me at the restaurant and that I'll have more free time to spend with her and the kids once she gets home. I'm also planning a long weekend away for the two of us when she's better, and this morning I arranged for Dad to have the kids. Four days away in early September, just the two of us. I'm not sure where we'll go yet but I want her to decide. We'll go wherever she wants. Paris. Barcelona. It's another expense we can't afford but there's always the credit card, and I can't remember the last time we spent quality time alone, just the two of us. It's the little things that mean so much.

But as I get through the next double doors that lead onto Jessie's ward, I can hear yelling and get a horrible sense that something is wrong. I stop and listen. It's Jessie's voice I can hear, followed by a gruff man's voice and then another more hushed voice that sounds like they're trying to calm the situation. I can't make out what anyone is saying, but I know it isn't good. I rush through the atrium that leads down to Jessie's room but stop as I get to the main doorway of the ward. A uniformed police officer is standing outside Jessie's room. She doesn't see me and, as I wait, frozen on the spot, two people shuffle out of the room. One is Jessie's doctor, a pleasant but serious woman called Dr Varma. The other is a tall man. He's dressed in a dark blue overcoat and I recognise him straight away. DCI Finlay.

No, Jessie.

What have you done?

I don't make a conscious decision to walk towards them, yet I find myself moving down the corridor. It feels as if I'm floating or having an out-of-body experience. As I get closer, Dr Varma sees me and rushes over with a concerned frown creasing her round face.

"Mr Wilkes," she says. "I was just telling these police officers that they cannot be here. They are upsetting your wife and I can't have it."

I smile weakly and nod. I don't know what else to do. I feel as if time has stopped. Somewhere I can hear a baby crying. It's Noah.

"Mr Wilkes," DCI Finlay says, moving around the side of Dr Varma. "Can I have a word?"

"Umm. Yes," I say, looking from him to Dr Varma and back again. "What's going on?"

He places his hand on my back between my shoulders and guides me down the corridor a few steps. "We had a phone call this morning, Mr Wilkes. From your wife." He speaks in a low voice, but I can't tell if it's driven by concern or just another feature of his hackneyed Columbo routine. "She spoke to one of my colleagues, but I've just been in with her now and she confirmed to me what she told them."

"Which is what?" I ask, staring at the square of scuffed lino under my feet. "What did she say?"

Finlay clears his throat. "That she's remembered something important. Apparently, your friend Daniel Chapman was trying to get money out of you, in a threatening manner. Is that correct?"

"What?" The walls rush in at me. I feel sick and dizzy, and I don't want to be here. "It wasn't that bad but—"

"She also said she remembers going to see Mr Chapman," Finlay cuts in, "and that she found him asleep in his sleeping bag. She said she then found a rock and hit him around the head at least six times. Enough to know he was dead."

I don't answer as the floor tilts away from me.

What do I do?

What do we do?

"Do you understand what I'm telling you, Mr Wilkes?" Finlay goes on. "Your wife has just confessed to the murder of Daniel Chapman."

I open my mouth and close it again. This happens at
least twice before I can form any words or even
draw a breath.

"She's... She's not well," I splutter, at last. "She's delusional and confused. Did Dr Varma not tell you this? She
doesn't know what she's saying."

"We are concerned about the validity of the confession, given your wife's condition. But the doctor has
confirmed she has improved a lot since she was admitted
and she appears to be making lucid decisions for herself."
He releases a low groan as if he has more to say. But of
course he does. He's a bleeding Columbo wannabe. "The
thing is, Mr Wilkes, we've also had a sighting of your
wife's car parked up in a lay-by near to where Daniel
Chapman was camped out on the afternoon of the twenty-
seventh. This fits with the estimated time of death.
Someone also saw a person – wearing a coat like the one
hanging in Mrs Wilkes' room – climbing up the hillside at
that time."

"That doesn't mean anything. She could have been

going for a walk in the fresh air. She does that often. A lot
of people who live around here do. Her walking near to
where Dan was camped doesn't mean she killed him."
DCI Finlay holds up his hands and I realise I've been
shouting. I let my shoulders drop. "She didn't even know
Dan was up there." That was in fact a question I'd not
been able to find an answer to myself, and I probably
never would. I most certainly wasn't planning on asking
Jessie. Maybe he'd told her, maybe she'd seen my van
there. Anyway, it didn't matter.

"Hmm," Finlay responds, with a hammy scowl. "I'm
afraid there's more, Mr Wilkes. Your wife claims she took
a notebook from Mr Chapman's tent and that there are
bloody fingerprints on it. Her fingerprints. His blood."

The bones in my legs feel as if they've dissolved. It's all
I can do to stay upright. "Again, she's delusional," I say.
"She doesn't know what she's saying."

"Well, this is easily solved," he says. "She told my
colleague this notepad was at your father's house, in a
drawer in his spare room. We'll be able to retrieve it once
we reopen the case."

Dark thoughts flood my mind as the adrenaline rises
in my system. "Wha-What will happen?" I stutter.

"We'll have to take Mrs Wilkes in for questioning
when she's deemed mentally fit." He moves around so
we're standing face to face and leans down to make eye
contact. "The thing is, Mr Wilkes, she was ill when this
happened. No one is disputing that. At worst she'll get a
suspended sentence due to diminished responsibility. But
she has admitted to the crime, and the times and sightings
do make sense, so we have to pursue this with the full
strength of the law. It will be handled sympathetically,
though. You have my word."

He smiles and I almost burst into tears. I can't do this. She can't do it. She was on the mend. What if this knocks her back? She could spend the rest of her life in and out of the hospital like my mum was. Or in some secure unit for the criminally insane. I don't know whether my imagination is running riot, but I can't deal with that idea. I can't have Jessie branded a psycho.

I think of my mum and my dad. I think of everything Dad did for me, everything he put up with and gave up for his family. I want to be more like him, and that starts right now. I'm aware I'm going to lose my freedom and maybe my sanity, but I'm also starkly aware suddenly that I lost both those things a long time ago.

For my family, I have to do the right thing. Jessie will get better, and the kids need her more than they do me. They need their mum. Even if it went to court and she got off with a plea of temporary insanity, it will plague her. With social media and the like, everyone knows everyone else's secrets.

No.

I won't have that for her. Or my children.

Dad protected me and made my mum a saint in my eyes. I have to do the same for my kids. Jessie and they can move away and start again. And I'd rather they hate me than her.

It's only what my dad would do in this situation.

Besides, I've been running from my past for too long. It's time to stop running. No more secrets.

"It's gone," I say.

DCI Finlay gives me a genuine frown. "Excuse me?"

"The notebook," I tell him. "I found it and I burnt it. It's gone."

"I see. Well, that does then implicate you also in—"

I glare at him. "I killed Dan Chapman," I say. "I did it, not Jessie. Either she's not as well as the doctors think or she's trying to cover for me. But either way, this is the truth. I killed Dan up on the hillside. He was trying to blackmail me, and I couldn't take it any longer. It's true that Jessie knew about it, but she wasn't involved. I went up there alone and found him asleep in his tent, in his sleeping bag, and I got a rock and I killed him. Then I threw the rock in the Torside Reservoir and brought the journal home to burn in our log burner. Jessie saw me doing it and I confessed to her what I'd done. I think that might be what sent her over the edge." I gasp as tears flood my eyes, but this isn't part of the act. I can see in Finlay's face that he's changing his mind. I suspect the grim details help my case. "And I drove Jessie's car to go see Dan," I continue. "That's why it was seen in the lay-by. And I left without a coat, so I put hers on. It was on the back seat."

I wait for him to reply, and it seems as though he's never going to. But I'm shocked at how good I feel after saying what I've said. It's as if the darkness has left me. I'm aware it's most likely another surge of adrenaline causing these feelings, rather than the abdication of guilt, but I feel liberated. I feel strong. I am the husband Jessie needs. I will shoulder this for her. I will fall on my sword.

"Mr Wilkes..." Finlay sighs and a quiver of nervous energy shoots up my body. "I can appreciate that you want to protect your wife. But I'm rather puzzled by this revelation. Does her coat even fit you?"

No.

He's not buying it.

In a second, I know what I have to do. All reason and logic drop away and it's just me, alone, fighting for my wife's innocence. I have to make this count. I have to make him believe me. I take a deep breath.

No more secrets...

No more running...

"There's a reason why I had to kill Dan Chapman," I tell him. "And it concerns the body you found in the reservoir."

Finlay leans back and regards me with a quizzical look. "Mr Wilkes. What are you saying?"

"I'm going to say goodbye to my wife, then I think you should take me to the station," I tell him. "We've got a lot to talk about."

THANK YOU FOR READING

Did you enjoy reading *The Secrets We Keep*? Please consider leaving a review on Amazon. Your review will help other readers to discover the novel.

ABOUT THE AUTHOR

M. I. Hattersley was born in Yorkshire. Over the last twenty years he has toured Europe in a rock 'n roll band, trained as a professional actor and founded a theatre and media company. He's also had many incredibly boring jobs to help sustain his creative endeavours.

Now he writes psychological and domestic thrillers and, as Matthew Hattersley, is a bestselling author of action thrillers.

He lives with his wife and daughter in Derbyshire and is not too comfortable writing about himself in third person.

www.mihattersley.com